DANNY ORLIS
AND THE
MEXICAN
KIDNAPPING

DANNY ORLIS
AND THE
MEXICAN KIDNAPPING

BERNARD PALMER

Danny Orlis and the Mexican Kidnapping
© 2024 by Bernard Palmer
All rights reserved. First edition 1971.
Second edition 2024.

Please do not reproduce, store in a retrieval system, or transmit in any form or by any means – electronic, mechanical, photocopying, recording, or otherwise, without written permission from the publisher.

Scripture quotations from The Authorized (King James) Version. Rights in the Authorized Version in the United Kingdom are vested in the Crown. Reproduced by permission of the Crown's patentee, Cambridge University Press.

Cover image: Adobe Firefly
Character illustrations: John Ball
Editor: Charlene Miskimen

Aneko Press Youth

www.anekopress.com

Aneko Press, Life Sentence Publishing, and our logos are trademarks of Life Sentence Publishing, Inc.
203 E. Birch Street
P.O. Box 652
Abbotsford, WI 54405

JUVENILE FICTION / Religious / Christian / Action & Adventure
Paperback ISBN: 979-8-88936-066-7
eBook ISBN: 979-8-88936-067-4
10 9 8 7 6 5 4 3 2 1
Available where books are sold

CONTENTS

CHAPTER 1

MEXICO BOUND!

Mack Flores stood outside the Roper ranch house, shifting uneasily from one bare foot to the other. Concern clouded his thin, brown face and flickered ominously in his eyes. He didn't know why he felt that he had to write to his cousins and his aunts and uncles back in his home village in Mexico.

He hadn't written to any of them since he and his brothers and sisters and their mother left for Texas. He hadn't even thought about them for months. Now it seemed that he was compelled to write that very night.

It wouldn't be an ordinary letter either, just telling what he had been doing and asking them how they were. He had to write and tell them what had happened to him. He had to explain how he had confessed his sin and had given his heart to God.

He had to make them understand how important it was and what a difference it had made in his life.

Mama had always talked to him and the little ones about religion and being good, but this was different. Like Mr. Roper said, Jesus Christ had given him a new life and was helping him to live the way he should.

In Sunday school the Sunday before, the lesson had been about hell and what it was going to be like. Mack sure didn't want any of his family to go there. But that was where they were all going unless someone told them about Jesus Christ and that He loved them enough to die on the cross for them.

That night he went down to the barn alone and crawled up into the haymow where he knelt and talked to God about it. He told Him that no one had ever gone to The Congregation of the Bulls (which was the name of his village) to tell the people about Jesus Christ.

"Please, dear God, send a preacher or a missionary or somebody down to our village to tell everybody about Jesus. They don't hear about Him there."

For the next several nights he prayed about the same thing, but it seemed as though God didn't hear his prayer. With each passing day his discouragement increased until, finally, he decided that he would write a letter to them. Why hadn't he thought of that before? Elation rushed over and shook hands with him.

Only he wasn't sure that he knew what to say. He

read the Bible regularly as he had been told to, every night and morning, but he didn't think he understood it well enough to explain it to anyone else. There were too many things he had to write down and ask Mr. Roper about.

That was it! Phil Roper's dad understood more about the Bible than anyone else on the ranch, except maybe Mrs. Roper. He would go to Mr. Roper and get him to write the letter, explaining everything the way he explained it in Sunday school. Mack might have to translate it into Spanish, but that wouldn't be hard once his employer set it down on paper.

Now he was at the Roper's back door, waiting for an answer to his knock. He rapped the casing again, sharply, and stepped back. A moment later he heard brisk footsteps approaching, and the kitchen door opened.

"Oh, it's you, Mack," Clarence Roper said. "Come on in."

"I'd like to talk to you." He squirmed nervously and inched backward as though he was about to leave. It was foolishness to ask a man as busy as his mother's employer to write a letter for him. But the rancher held the screen door open and motioned for him to come inside.

"Sure thing. The boys are out riding fence and it's terribly quiet around the house with Carmen and Maria away. I'm so lonely I'm about to climb the walls."

Mack couldn't keep from snickering. That would be something to see – Mr. Roper climbing the walls like a squirrel! He was glad he had decided to come.

They went into the living room and sat down. Finally Mack blurted out the reason for his visit.

"And so I thought maybe you would write a letter to them for me, one that will explain all about Jesus and how He loves them and has a plan for their lives."

Mr. Roper's big fists opened and closed nervously.

"I don't write Spanish, Mack. I speak a little and can read some, but I never did learn to write it."

"When you finish," Mack continued, caught up with the excitement of his plan, "I can translate it into Spanish. I would write the letter to them myself, but–" He gestured helplessly. "I don't know what to say."

Clarence sympathized with that. He could get up and talk without much trouble, but he always had hated to put words down on paper. Carmen did the correspondence for the family. When she got back, she could handle the letter for Mack. She wouldn't have any problems, even in Spanish.

But Mack hadn't asked *her* to write the letter. Mack had come to *him*. And it was something a guy shouldn't wait about. It ought to be written right away.

"I'll see what I can do, Mack," he said evasively. "Come back and see me tomorrow or the next day. I'll have something ready for you."

"Gracias."

With that the boy was gone, leaving Clarence alone

in the big, rambling house. He remained at the door until his young visitor disappeared into the cook's house where he lived with his mother and the little ones. Then, with marked reluctance, he went back to his desk, got his Bible, and opened it.

Writing a letter ought to be as easy as speaking, he reasoned. He would decide what he'd say if he was actually at The Congregation of the Bulls talking with Mack's relatives, and then he would put the words on paper. It was as simple as that.

Only it wasn't so simple. He tried a dozen times to get the letter started, but the words would not come. He was still at it when his son, Phil, and his cousins, Del and Doug Davis, rode into the yard and unsaddled.

"Writing to Mom and Maria?" Phil asked when he and the Davis boys came into the house a few minutes later.

Clarence shook his head. "I promised Mack I'd write a letter for him, and, believe me, I'm having plenty of trouble."

He told them about Mack's visit and the reason for it.

"We could take Mack down to his old village, Dad," Phil suggested, "and let him talk to them himself."

"It'd sure be a lot easier than trying to write a letter for him."

Phil had only been kidding when he suggested going down to Mexico, and Clarence hadn't seriously considered it. That night, however, he began to think about it, and it didn't seem preposterous at all. He would never make a trip in order to keep from writing a letter. That would be ridiculous. But he had been thinking seriously about taking the boys on a vacation. It was so lonely around the ranch without Carmen and Maria for one thing, and for another, the three of them had been working so hard he wanted to reward them. He had been considering a trip to Houston to see a couple of baseball games. Going down into Mexico to help Mack try to reach his own family sounded more exciting to him than any baseball game. And he thought the boys would enjoy it more too. The next morning he talked with them about it.

"What do you think?" he concluded at the breakfast table after laying his plan before them.

"It sounds great!" Del said. "When can we start south?"

"We've got some plans to make first and a little more work to do around here."

Before they left the house to ride fence once more, everything was set up. Clarence wrote for some Spanish New Testaments to give away and got off a letter to his wife and daughter, telling them of the change in plans. Only then did he call Mack in to tell him about the trip.

The boy thought he wanted to talk about the letter he was going to write for him.

"Did you get it finished yet?" he asked, his voice betraying his concern.

"Not exactly."

"But you are going to write it for me, no?" he asked.

"I said I would," Clarence continued, keeping the smile from his lips. "But I changed my mind. It's too tough for me to write a letter. I never know what to say. That's all right, isn't it?"

The clouds came back to Mack's eyes, threatening rain.

"I–I guess so."

The lad was so dejected, so forlorn in his hopelessness that Clarence was sorry he teased him.

"I was talking with Phil and Doug and Del," he said, "and we came up with an idea that's a lot better than writing a dozen letters." He reached over, impulsively, and rumpled Mack's shining black hair. "We decided we'd take you and go down to The Congregation of the Bulls so you can tell your family there about Jesus Christ and what He's done for you."

Mack's eyes rounded in surprise, and he was so stunned by Mr. Roper's announcement that he had difficulty speaking for a minute. Slowly, he began to understand what the rancher was trying to tell him.

"Do you mean you're going to take me down to Mexico to see my cousins and aunts and uncles?" he wanted to know. "You aren't joking, are you?"

"I've never been more serious in my life."

Mack considered the news briefly. "And what about Mama and the little ones? Will they get to go, too?"

"We'd like to take them, Mack, but I'm afraid there won't be room."

"I think maybe Mama wants to stay here on the ranch, anyway." Excitement flashed in his dark eyes. "I'll go and talk to her and see if I can go."

"There's no need for that," Clarence said genially. "I already talked with her. She said she'll be glad to be rid of you for a couple of weeks."

* * *

Leaving a cattle ranch as large as the Circle-R, even for a couple of weeks, was not simple. The foreman had to be briefed once more on every operation of the vast spread, supplies of feed and medication had to be checked, and the fences had to be ridden to make sure there were no breaks.

Phil, Del, and Doug had been working on the fence for the past week, but now that they were planning a trip that would take them away for at least two weeks, Clarence wanted to be sure that every foot of fence would be gone over. The boys rode out before daylight and didn't come in at night until the sun was hiding behind the barren rim of the prairie.

And that was not all. The trip wasn't going to be on the main roads where there were modern motels to stay in and good cafes to patronize. They were going back into the hills where tourists never got to go. They had to have their own tents and sleeping bags and grub along.

That was one of the things that made the trip so exciting for Doug and Del and their cousin, Phil.

"I'm glad we're going to be able to 'rough it' a little," Del said. "I don't like having to stay in fancy motels all the time."

"Mack says we'll have to have our own tents if we want a place to stay," Phil put in. "I guess there's no chance of even getting a meal at the village where he used to live unless one of the families would take pity on us."

"It's going to be more fun cooking for ourselves, anyway."

By the time the Spanish New Testaments arrived, the boys and Mr. Roper had everything ready. Their tents and sleeping bags were in the car along with their grub box. The boys helped carry the six boxes of New Testaments to the car and put them inside.

"What're we going to do with all of these Bibles?" Doug wanted to know.

"I thought it would be good to have something to give to the people," Clarence told him. "Even if they don't listen to us, the Testaments can speak to their hearts."

"Maybe they won't even take them," Del said. "I'll bet we have a lot of trouble getting rid of all we're taking along."

Mack spoke up. "Oh, they'll take them, all right. Everybody in Mexico likes to have such nice books."

There was something else that troubled Doug. He didn't want it to sound as though he was afraid, but it was the sort of thing that made a guy wonder.

"I thought it was against the law to give out Bibles to anyone in Mexico."

Mack Flores and Phil Roper stared at him, questions gleaming in their eyes.

"Against the law?" Phil echoed. "Why would it be against the law to give something away? Dad bought the Bibles and paid for them. They belong to him. He ought to be able to give them away if he wants to."

The Davis boy was still not satisfied with their explanation. "When we were living in Guatemala before Dad and Mom were drowned, a missionary to Mexico stopped to visit us. I heard Dad and him talking about some trouble he'd gotten into in Mexico City, and I thought he was talking about being arrested for giving gospels of John away."

"You must be wrong about that, Doug," Mack said firmly. "I lived in Mexico all my life until I came up here to Texas, and I never heard anything like that."

"Maybe it isn't that way anymore," Phil replied. "They must have changed that law, if there ever was one like that."

"Let's *hope* they've changed it," Del put in. "I sure don't want to go to any jail in Mexico."

"Neither do the rest of us," Phil said, laughing.

Mack Flores ate with the Ropers and Doug and Del that night. At least he sat down at the table with them. He was so excited he could scarcely eat.

"Just think!" he exclaimed, his voice trembling with emotion. "By tomorrow night we'll be down in my village, maybe."

The rancher's grin spread across his broad, good-natured face. "I don't believe we can come up with quite such fast traveling time, Mack. But we ought to get well into Mexico by tomorrow night if everything goes well. And the next night we should be in The Congregation of the Bulls."

"No matter." Mack's eagerness was infectious. "We'll be there soon, and I'll get to see all of my old friends. Let's see, there's Eduardo and Carlos and Pepito and Alfredo–" He was counting his friends on his fingers. "They were my very best pals. And Pepito and Carlos are my cousins, too." The words stopped as suddenly as they had begun to gush out. Then he added, "And maybe I will get to tell them about Jesus and what He has done for me."

Clarence Roper's face was serious. "We've been praying that you'd get a chance to tell them what Jesus Christ has done for you, Mack. And I know He's going to give you that chance."

"Sí." He took a deep breath. "And when I talk to them, I hope they listen good and understand what I say to them."

CHAPTER 2

TROUBLE FROM THE START

The time arrived for them to leave the ranch for the Mexican village where Mack and his family used to live. Shortly after dawn, Mr. Roper and the boys finished breakfast and piled into the car. The rancher glanced at his son.

"Check the map, will you, Phil? Make sure it is set to the right place. We change highways a couple of times before we get on the Brownsville road."

"And we sure don't want to get lost," Doug added.

"Maybe *we'd* better look at the map instead of Phil," Del said, eyeing his cousin mischievously. "He can't even find his way around your south pasture without getting lost."

"Oh, hush. I'm not the one who insists on going the wrong way most of the time."

As they talked, Phil Roper looked at the map of their portion of Texas and began to study it intently.

There weren't too many roads in that area, and getting on the wrong one would take them miles and miles out of the way.

Del and Doug and Mack scooted forward until they were sitting on the edge of the back seat watching the flat, mesquite-dotted pastureland race by. Phil found the right road in spite of Del's ribbing. By noon they had reached Brownsville, cleared customs, and gone into Matamoras, Mexico. By the middle of the afternoon, they had crossed the barren, semidesert land and could see the mountains in the distance.

"Have you decided where we're going to stay for the night, Uncle Clarence?" Del asked.

The Texas rancher shook his head. "Not for sure. Maybe in Victoria if we can get that far tonight." He slowed to allow a donkey to saunter across the road in front of them. "That would leave us a comparatively short trip tomorrow."

It didn't take as long to reach Victoria as he thought it would. They were there shortly before four o'clock in the afternoon, pulling up to the market square and stopping.

"We aren't going to camp here, are we?" Mack asked seriously.

"We should be able to find a better place to camp than this," Mr. Roper said, seeing that the sidewalks were teeming with people. "There's sure a big crowd out this afternoon."

"It's always this way at the market."

Clarence removed the key from the ignition and got out of the car. "This looks like a good place to pass out some Bibles. How about it?"

"Sounds good to me," Mack exclaimed, his eyes brightening.

The boys piled out of the car, and Del went around to the back and opened the trunk. One man stopped to watch as the boys pulled a box of books out and Mr. Roper opened it with his jackknife. Another came to a halt beside the first, eyeing what was going on, curiously. Soon another stopped and another and another until they had a sizeable crowd around them.

"*Buenas dias,* señor," Doug said to the closest spectator. His Spanish was rusty, but he managed to make himself understood. "Would you like to have a free book?"

Suspicion appeared in the handsome young Mexican's face. "What kind of a book?" he wanted to know.

"It is God's book, señor. He tells us what we are like and what we can do to be changed so we can go to heaven."

The stranger started on, but stopped and turned back, picking up the Testament curiously. "And what do I have to pay for this book?"

"Nothing. It is free. All you have to do is take it home with you."

This the Mexican could not understand. "I have

never owned a book in my whole life. What do I have to *do* to get it?"

Laboriously Doug explained again that all he had to do was to promise to read it. That seemed to resolve the man's doubts.

"I will take it, señor. Gracias."

Clarence, who could also speak a little Spanish, was talking with another young man about the age of the man Doug had been talking to. He, too, had to be assured that the books were free and that they didn't have to work for them or anything. Moments later the two of them went down the street carrying their New Testaments proudly.

Others saw that the two young men had been given books without charge and stepped forward, asking Mr. Roper or one of the boys for a book of their own. The hesitation and skepticism that was so apparent in the first two spectators was not visible in the others. They crowded about the car clamoring for books.

That was the situation when the police approached. They were making a routine patrol past the Roper car when they saw the size of the crowd gathered there and whipped over to the curb. They did not get out of their car immediately but watched what was going on.

Del Davis saw them and nudged his brother with his elbow. "Don't look now, but I think we're about to have company."

"What's so bad about that? We've got all kinds of company here right now."

"You're not going to like this company," Del whispered.

Doug could not resist turning so he could see what was disturbing his brother so much. His throat tightened as he saw the officers.

"Jailhouse, here we come," he whispered under his breath.

While he watched, one of the officers got out of the car and touched a ragged boy eleven or twelve years old on the arm. "What is it?" he asked sternly. What's going on here to cause such a crowd?"

"It is the books they're giving away."

"For free?" the officer asked.

"Sí, señor. And I am going to get one, too."

"What kind of books do the Americanos give away?" he persisted.

The boy shrugged his shoulders. "Red ones, I guess."

"They do not make anyone pay?" he repeated, his tone revealing that he had difficulty believing what the boy had said. "They do not charge anything for them?"

"Sí, that is the way it is. I have watched them. They do not take money for the books." He edged forward. "I am going to get one, too, if they do not run out before–before I get to them." The boy left the officer's side and began to push his way through the crowd.

The officer went back to his partner, talked with

him briefly, and turned back to the crowd once more. This time his companion joined him.

Mr. Roper, Phil, and Mack hadn't noticed the police until they were almost on them. Mack leaned closer to Doug. "Here comes the army."

"That's what Del and I have been trying to tell you, but you've all been so busy you wouldn't listen to us."

"What do we do now?" Mack asked under his breath. "Make a run for it?"

"That would get us into trouble."

"We're already in a mess if you ask me."

Before anyone could answer Mack, one of the police officers approached Mr. Roper and spoke roughly to him.

"And just what are you doing here?" he demanded sternly.

The lanky Texan looked up, calm and quiet in spite of the fact that the man who addressed him was an officer. "We're giving New Testaments away. Would you like one?"

"Testaments? And what is a Testament?" That was what he would like to know.

His companion spoke quickly. "You know – Testaments. Religious books."

The first uniformed man's face grew stern, and his voice took on a tone of accusation. "Religious books?" he echoed. "It is against the law, señor, to give religious books to the people. We can have you in jail for that."

Clarence Roper was still not disturbed. A faint smile lit his face briefly. "You must be mistaken, officer. These books belong to me. I bought and paid for them. Surely, I can do what I want to with them, can't I?"

"But did you pay customs to bring them in at the border? Did you declare to the officials what you planned to do with these books?" questioned the officer arrogantly.

"No one at the border asked about them. I did not hide them."

"No matter, señor. If you did not declare them and pay customs, then it is against the law, and you must leave here now. You could be deported or maybe even spend a long time in jail."

Clarence Roper continued in his efforts to persuade the officers that giving out the Bibles did not break the law but without success. The officers were as determined to stop the distribution as he was to continue it. At last the police spokesman's voice was stern and decisive.

"Enough! The streets are not the place to give religious books away. You pack up and go, Señor Americano," he demanded, "and we forget what you do this time. But if you give away one more book – just one – I will put you all in jail! And you would not like that, señor, believe me."

"You've got a point there," Clarence said, recognizing that the time had come for him to retreat before the officers made good their threat. "We'll go. We'll go!"

The boys, who had been listening to the heated discussion, closed the box of New Testaments they had just opened, shoved it into the back, and closed the trunk. Once that was accomplished they climbed hurriedly into the vehicle, and Mr. Roper started the engine. They were pulling out into the line of traffic when Phil turned to his dad.

"That was close!"

"You can say that again!" Mack exclaimed. A moment later he directed his attention to Doug. "I guess you were right when you said that it was against the law to distribute Bibles here in my country."

"I should have checked with some high official source before we came," Clarence said regretfully. "It could be that those officers are just against any other religion than their own and didn't want us to stay in their town. I've heard about things like this, but I've never seen them. It's really sad, isn't it? We have so many Bibles and they have so few."

Doug Davis, who had been so concerned about the officers that he kept looking back, half afraid that they might have changed their minds and were racing after the car to arrest them, leaned forward.

"Uncle Clarence," he said tensely, "I think we're being followed."

"Followed?" Mr. Roper's big laugh boomed.

"And who would want to follow us?"

"The police, maybe?"

"The police aren't going to bother us. If they are following us, it's only to be sure that we go on out of town and don't stop to give away any more Testaments."

"There's somebody following us, Uncle Clarence," Del said. "And that's for sure. They've been behind us almost all the way from the market."

By this time everyone in the car (with the exception of the driver) was staring out the back window, staring at the traffic behind them.

"It isn't a police car, Dad," Phil said. "I can tell you that much. The car isn't even halfway in repair. It's an old red and white klunker that looks as though it's about to fall apart."

"Maybe the people in it got a Testament and want to talk to us," Mack suggested.

"And maybe not," Del replied laconically. "I don't think we'd get results like that so soon."

Clarence wasn't really concerned about the old car the boys said was following them, he told himself. The chances were that it just happened that the two cars left the market about the same time and were going in the same direction. Nevertheless, he didn't like the idea of making camp when there was any possibility that someone was following them.

Without saying anything to the boys he began to look for motel signs. Only when he saw one that looked adequate and he was slowing to turn in did he tell the boys what he had in mind.

"How about going in here?" he asked.

"A motel?" Mack asked, disappointment obvious in his voice. "I thought we were going to camp out."

"We will. I can promise you that. But I thought it would be nice for us to have good beds for tonight and get well rested before we go on to your village."

"It sounds great to me," Del said. "I don't much like the idea of sleeping out after seeing those guys who were following us. It gives me the creeps."

"Nobody would want to follow us," Clarence said, laughing.

He stopped the car, got out, and went into the motel office while the boys waited in the car.

"I wish we knew what's going on," Doug said softly. "That's what I wish."

"Probably nothing," Del said.

"Oh, yeah? For your information that old car's coming by again!"

Del's breath caught in his mouth. "Are you sure?" he managed.

"Of course, I'm sure. Take a look for yourself!"

CHAPTER 3

AND MORE TROUBLE TO COME

While the boys stared, the battered, old car crawled past the motel and disappeared from view.

"Do you suppose the guys in that car are really looking for us?" Del asked.

"If they were, they must not have wanted us very bad. They didn't even stop."

"No, but they came by again." He lowered his voice ominously. "You can't make me change my mind about that. I'm convinced that they're following us."

"I still say they could have stopped if they'd wanted us very bad. Look where we're parked." He gestured quickly. "We're out in the open where anybody who wanted to see us could do so. Uncle Clarence didn't make any effort to hide the car."

They were still discussing the matter when the red and white car with the battered fenders and cracked windshield came by again, inching along.

"There they are again!" Mack's voice caught in his throat.

"What do you suppose they're doing?" Phil whispered. This time his voice revealed his concern.

Doug was the only one who wasn't particularly disturbed. "If you ask me, they drove around the block to see some girls on the street, or maybe they're looking for a place to park. There could be a lot of reasons why they would drive around the block again."

Mack followed the tortuous progress of the old car along the busy street until it finally disappeared from view.

"You know," he said, trying unsuccessfully to hide his own concern, "I wish the police were the ones who were following us. At least if it was the cops, we wouldn't have to be afraid of them."

"If we've stopped giving away Testaments," Phil added. "If we keep that up, the chances are that we'll wind up in jail."

Del had been thinking about the old car. "Do you suppose the cops down here would use an old car like that to keep us from knowing that they're after us?" he asked. "Maybe they use that when they don't want anyone to know they're around?"

"I suppose that could be," Phil said doubtfully, "but it doesn't sound reasonable to me. I don't think they'd care whether we knew they were on our trail or not. They've already got evidence that we broke the law. They wouldn't have to prove it again. All they'd have to do is arrest us."

Doug considered the matter thoughtfully. *Maybe what Phil said was right. It did seem to make sense. Why would the police try to disguise their car when it wasn't necessary? On the other hand, why would anyone else be following us? And especially, why would anyone in an old wreck of a car want to spy on us? The question kept coming back to torment him. Why? Why? Why?*

The more he pondered it, the more confused he became. When it came right down to it, they didn't know for sure that the car they had just seen was the one that had been following them. It could have been a coincidence that they saw two cars that looked so very much alike. There were a lot of old cars in Victoria, the same as anywhere else.

Still, he had to admit that just thinking about it made him uneasy. He had that vague feeling that the men in the old car were actually following them. It didn't make sense, but then, there were many things that didn't make sense to him.

There had to be some logical explanation for the old car being behind them. There was no real reason for anyone trying to follow them. They certainly weren't rich, so robbery couldn't be the motive behind it. And it wasn't because of where they were going. Doug was sure that nine out of ten people in the city didn't even know there was such a village as The Congregation of the Bulls. So it couldn't be that the men in the old car were trying to keep them from getting to the village that was their destination.

The only thing Doug could think of that even began to make sense was the fact that the men in the old car had seen the Testament distribution and had gotten curious about it.

Maybe they wanted to get copies of the Testament for themselves and were following the car in the hope that they would catch up with it and get books. Doug sort of hoped that that wasn't the reason, or at least he hoped they wouldn't come barging in and ask Clarence for copies of the book they had been distributing. He thought he knew his uncle well enough to know that he would likely give them Testaments if they asked, and then they would all be in trouble with the police again.

He was still going over those things in his mind when Phil's dad came out and got in the driver's seat once more. "Well, we'll be staying here tonight. How does that sound?"

"Sounds great to me," Del said.

"Me too," his brother added. "But let's take rooms on the back away from the street. Okay?"

The rancher squinted at him. "Don't tell me that you're afraid all the traffic will keep you awake?"

Doug laughed nervously. "Not exactly." How could he tell Uncle Clarence that it was those two men in the old car that were concerning him?

"We're getting the only rooms they have left," Clarence said, "and they're all on the street, but I don't think the traffic will be enough to bother any of us."

* * *

Half an hour later the old red and white car with Texas license plates crept slowly past the motel for the fourth time.

"Do you see 'em, Gonzales?" the red-haired driver drawled.

"No, Señor Red. I do not see them anymore. They are gone! Vanish!" He gestured wildly. "One minute they are here, and I am sure they stay at least for the night. Then – poof! They are here no more!"

"They can't disappear so quick! They've got to be somewhere!"

"Sí, they have to be somewhere. But tell me, señor, where is this *somewhere* you keep talking about? How do we find it?"

"Just our luck!" Red swore under his breath and turned left to go around the block once more.

They were back on the highway that led south and were about to approach the motel once more when the thin-faced Gonzales spoke.

"And what do we do now?" There was disgust in his voice. "Do we go around again? You must remember, we have no more pesos for extra gasoline mañana. You forget that, señor?"

Red Sanford snorted his disgust, as though men like himself should not have to be bothered with such common matters as money.

"Those guys *had* to go someplace, Juan. And if they went someplace, we can find them – if it takes a month."

"Only they won't be here a month, señor. The chances are that they go on the first thing in the morning."

"We'll find them," Red muttered darkly. "That's all that matters."

Juan's eyes widened. "But why?" he asked innocently. "What do we do when we find them?"

"What do we do?" The words exploded from Red's lips. "You saw 'em givin' those books away, didn't you?"

"Sí, but I–"

"Don't you get it? They're rich! They've got so much money they buy things and give them away! So, we're going to get them to give us some of that money."

"Do you think they will?"

"You stupid ox! They won't do it on purpose – no! But they have plenty of money. We'll figure some way to get it from them."

Juan thought about that. The Americano and the boys who were with him were giving out books, that was true. And he had never known anyone to give things away before. But then, he had never seen a rich Americano before.

"You think maybe they give us some books? No?"

Red snorted his indignation. "No, I don't think 'maybe they give us some books.' If I'd wanted one of their books, I'd have gone up and gotten one." He frowned. "That guy's from Texas. The chances are that he's a millionaire oil man."

Now that was something Juan had not even considered. But then, how would he know about such things? He had not been more than a few miles from his village all his life until he stole a farmer's cow and had been thrown in jail in Matamoras. There, in the class where they taught them English, he had met Red Sanford, who had gotten into some kind of trouble below the border and was also sent to prison.

Juan had never learned why Red was there, but it didn't matter. The two men became good friends. And one day when they were working on the prison farm, the guard turned his back. It was only long enough for him to light a cigarette, but they could not resist running away.

Red wanted to cross the border into Texas and had Juan talked into going with him, but almost at the bridge they saw a police car and lost their nerve. Instead, they turned in the opposite direction.

"I just thought of something!" the American said. "I've got my old car around here somewhere – if somebody hasn't swiped it. We'll find it and go south in style."

They located the car easily. It was still in the care

of a Mexican friend who hadn't driven it because he didn't want to buy gasoline. Red had no money for gas or the new battery he needed. But when he could not talk his friend into loaning the money to him, he went out at night, got a battery from another old car, and broke the lock on somebody's gas barrel to fill the tank. The next morning he was able to sell two stolen tires for enough to give them a few pesos for food, and they were on their way. They dabbed the Texas license with mud in an effort to keep the inquisitive from knowing it was three years old, and they started south. Now they were in Victoria, almost at the end of both their pesos and their gasoline. The car with its wealthy occupants was their only hope of avoiding disaster – or so they reasoned.

"What good does it do for the señor in the big car to be an oil man?" Juan asked. "Answer me that."

Red gripped the wheel tightly and went over the matter aloud. His plan was only half formed in his mind.

"Maybe he's got a bundle of that money on him, and you and I can get it away from him."

"How do we do that?"

Sanford shook his head. Sometimes it seemed that Juan didn't know anything. "We'll steal it, of course."

His Mexican friend eyed him sorrowfully. "But I no have experience stealing money."

"Don't give me that. They had you locked up for it. I saw it on your record – grand larceny."

"I steal, sí. But I have only experience at cow stealing. And the only time I do that I get caught, señor!"

Red snorted. "A lot of help you're going to be."

"But I will try, señor. You tell me what to do and I will try to be a good thief."

"At least you're willing. That's something." He guided the old car around the next corner with a practiced hand. "We'll think of something. But right now we've got to find them or we're out of luck. If we don't, we're whipped! Ruined! The cops'll have us back in Matamoras before the end of the week."

"No, señor!" Juan spoke quickly. "They don't do that to us! We find the rich Americano. We steal from him, no?"

At that instant he glanced ahead and to the left. There was the car from Texas parked in front of the motel.

"Señor Red!" Excitedly he grabbed his companion's elbow. "There it is! There's the car we look for! We've found him!"

Red Sanford jerked away, swerving as he did so. He almost had a head-on collision with an oncoming car. Sweat popped out on his forehead, and he chewed nervously on his lower lip.

"Dummy!" he growled under his breath. "See what you almost made me do! Ain't you got a lick of sense, Juan?"

His Mexican friend was too excited to understand

what he was saying. "I see the car, señor!" he cried again. "I see it! Over there!"

Red swore at him. "Keep up that yelling and everybody in Victoria will know it. What do you want me to do? Go to the police station and let you yell to them that you see the Americano's car? The car that belongs to the rich Americano, the one we are going to rob?"

Juan's lips quivered. "But you say you want to find them, señor. You say it do us no good unless we find where they are. Now I have see them."

Before Sanford could reply, the wheezing engine coughed spasmodically. Both men jerked up. "What you do, Señor Red? What happen?"

"What did I do?" Sanford's voice raised. "What did I do? I didn't do nothin'! That's what I do! I was just sittin' here when–"

It happened again. This time the engine coughed and died.

"What happened?" Terror widened Juan's eyes. "What is wrong, señor?"

"We're out of gas! That's what has happened! And we don't have any money to get more, either."

Juan was disconsolate. "We just find the so-rich Americano and before we can steal his money – poof! We run out of gas! I tell you we use too much gas hunting for them. I warn you, señor!"

"Aw, shut up!"

CHAPTER 4

AN UNFRIENDLY MEETING

Juan Gonzales eyed his companion who was still behind the steering wheel of the old car.

"Now what we do, Señor Red?" he asked fearfully. "How we going to follow our rich Americano and get his money when the car she no go?"

Red Sanford shook his head. "I don't know why I put up with you, Gonzales. You don't know nothin'. We've got to get some gas right away before that guy decides to leave." Cars began to honk at the stalled vehicle, so the two men got out and pushed it off the road.

Juan nodded sagely. "Sí," he murmured as much to himself as to Sanford. "We got to get some gas – that I know. But how we get him? What we use for money?"

The driver, who was about to get back inside the car,

stopped with his hand on the door. The wrinkles in his forehead deepened and his eyes squinted seriously.

"I'm not sure about that, Gonzales. Maybe we'll have to steal some money – or some gas."

At that same moment Clarence Roper decided that it was time for him and the boys to go to a nearby café for dinner. As they left their rooms, Del saw the old car that was stopped almost directly across the street. He stopped suddenly and grasped his cousin by the arm.

"Look over there, Phil," he whispered. "Does that old car look familiar to you?"

Phil Roper stared at it. "That looks like the old car we thought was following us after we left the market this afternoon."

"That's right!" By this time, the rest of the little party was several paces ahead. "I'm sure that's the old car that followed us out here and then went around the block three or four times after we stopped to get rooms."

Phil squinted at his cousin. "What do you think we ought to do?"

"Let's go over and take a look, okay?"

"You guys go on ahead, Dad," Phil said aloud. "We'll be there in a jiffy."

Doug stopped and spun on his heel. He knew both his brother and his cousin, and he wasn't going to miss out on anything if he could help it.

"What are you guys going to do?"

Del put a warning finger to his lips and then motioned significantly in the direction of the stalled car and the two men leaning against the side of it. Doug gasped audibly.

"We'll be right with you," Del told him. "We've got something to do before we go over to the cafe."

Doug hesitated. He wasn't going on and let Phil and Del have all the fun. At least he didn't want to. But if he tried to join them, the chances were that Mack and Clarence Roper would get suspicious and no one would get to find out anything about that old car. Frowning, he followed his uncle and Mack Flores up the sidewalk and into the neat little cafe on the corner.

As soon as the others were gone, Phil and Del cut across the parking lot toward the old car.

"What do you suppose those guys are doing over there, anyway?" Phil said in low tones.

On the curb Del stopped for an instant. "I sure wouldn't know, but I've got a hunch that it's got something to do with us."

At the sound of voices Juan Gonzales looked up at the two boys approaching. "What you want, señors?" he demanded. When he spoke, his open mouth revealed the decayed snags that were his teeth.

Del answered him in broken Spanish. "We don't want anything. We saw your car here and figured you might need a little help, that's all."

"You hear that, Señor Red?" Gonzales exclaimed, turning quickly to his friend. "They want to help us."

Once more he directed his attention to the boys. "Sí. We could use a little gasoline."

Red Sanford gouged his companion in the ribs with his elbow. "Shut up, Gonzales! You'll ruin everything with your big mouth." He came up beside his Mexican friend and spoke to Del and Phil. "We don't need anything. Juan was just making a joke. He's a great joker, that one."

"But–" Gonzales protested.

"Shut up! I'll do the talking around here!"

He said something in a whisper that the boys didn't hear.

Juan took half a step forward, his fist drawn back as though he was about to use it. "Go on!" he snarled at the boys. "Beat it! If you know what is good for you, get out of here!"

"You don't need to get so worked up about it," Phil said as he and Del retreated hastily. "We're going."

"And don't you come back!" the tall one called Sanford exclaimed.

Once safely across the street the boys stopped and turned to see the two men still standing beside the car watching them intently.

"They sure aren't the most friendly guys in the world," Phil said.

"They sort of give a guy the idea they want to be left alone."

"Whatever made you think that?"

They both laughed nervously.

"The next time I get an idea as crazy as that one about going over to take a look at their old car, I hope somebody steps on me," Del said.

"Don't worry. I'll be the first." Just outside the cafe door they stopped. "They didn't act to me as though they're following anyone. I got the idea they just want to be left alone."

"Maybe, and maybe not." What Phil said made sense, that was true, but still Del wasn't satisfied. He still had the uneasy feeling that the two men in the old car had, indeed, been following them. Del was even more disturbed than he had been before. There was something about the looks of the men that made him realize they would be capable of doing most anything.

But once inside the cafe where everyone else was chattering excitedly, he forgot most of his concern.

The next morning when Clarence and the boys loaded their gear into the car again and Phil's dad flicked on the switch to start it, he noted the gauges.

"Hmmm," he murmured. "That's funny."

The boys were looking at him curiously. "What do you mean, Dad?" Phil asked.

"I thought I filled the car with gas after we got to Victoria."

"You did," Doug spoke up. "You said you wanted to be all ready to go this morning."

"That's what I thought, but the tank's almost empty now."

Phil and Del glanced knowingly at each other but said nothing.

"Well, our first stop is going to be a gas station."

They drove steadily that morning after filling with gas once more. At noon they stopped in a cafe just off the town square for a meal of tortillas and enchiladas. They were sitting at the table eating when Clarence began to talk about the gasoline that had been stolen from their car the night before.

"Somebody must have a lot of nerve, or they would never have dared to come that close to our window to steal the gas. I just wish I could have gotten my hands on them."

Phil swallowed against the lump in his throat, and his gaze met Del's.

"What's the matter?" his dad demanded quickly. "Do you guys know something about our missing tank of gasoline that I don't know?"

Del Davis colored. "Well–" He moistened his lips with the tip of his tongue. "Well, we sort of know who might have taken it."

Phil continued quickly before anyone else had a chance to say anything. "What Del means is that we saw these two guys in this old car when we were going to the cafe with you to eat. We got curious so we went over there and–and–"

He stopped and his cousin went on, breathlessly.

He told how they had gone over to the old car and how Gonzales said they needed gasoline.

"And then this skinny American told us his friend didn't know what he was talking about. The next thing we knew, we were ordered to go on our way and leave them alone."

Clarence nodded. "It was after dark when we went into the cafe to eat. I'll bet they didn't even wait until we were in bed. They probably slipped over here and stole our gas before we got out of the cafe."

Phil shuddered. "They're the kind of guys who would do most anything. I can tell you that much."

Clarence turned to his son. "Maybe we're fortunate that they stole our gas. If you'd said something about those guys at the time, Phil, we might have caught them in the act."

"If we'd known what we know now we probably would have. But we didn't even think about the fact that they might be wanting to steal something. We figured maybe they were following us, and we wanted to find out why."

"What gave you that idea?"

"We saw them tagging along behind us after we left the market," Phil went on. "And while you were in seeing about motel rooms, they drove by two or three times, so slow we thought they were going to stop. When we saw that, we figured they were trying to tail us."

Mr. Roper pulled at the lobe of his ear.

"You guys must've let your imaginations get away from you. What reason would they have for following us if they weren't going to steal something?"

"If they were following us," Mack Flores said, "we don't have to worry about them anymore. We're a long way from Victoria, and we haven't seen anything of them this morning."

Del squirmed in his chair, suddenly uncomfortable. He hadn't expected Uncle Clarence and the others to doubt him and Phil.

"You guys can talk that way if you want to, but you should've seen Gonzales and that other guy named Red. They're a couple of tough characters, believe me."

Doug, who had been staring idly out the window while everyone else was talking, half raised from his chair and caught his breath audibly.

"Now what's eatin' you?" Clarence asked, deliberately curtailing the concern that flared in his dark eyes.

"Yeah," Del exclaimed. "What's the matter?"

With difficulty his brother kept his voice low and controlled. "It was them!" he said softly. "They just went by in that old car!"

"You must be mistaken." Clarence managed to laugh at him. "You're getting as jumpy as Phil and that brother of yours."

"But it was them, Uncle Clarence. They had slowed down, and I got a real good look at them.

The American was driving and the other guy was sitting beside him."

"Are you sure?"

"Of course, I'm sure. It was that same old car that was parked across the street from our motel last night. I'd recognize that old wreck anywhere."

Fright stole the color from Mack's cheeks and put a tremor in his firm, young hands. He almost spilled the water in his glass as he set it back on the table.

"Why do you suppose they've come all the way down here, Mr. Roper?" he wanted to know. "Do you *really* think they're after us?"

The tall Texan laughed. "If you want to know what I believe, it's that three guys I know have been reading too many adventure stories. Things like this don't actually happen. Not in real life."

"I know what I saw," Doug protested doggedly.

"You thought you saw the same car, Doug," his uncle said. "I don't doubt that at all, but Mexico is full of old cars just like the States are. Detroit probably made half a million just like that one."

Doug Davis did not reply. How could he, in the face of his uncle's kindly scorn? But he hadn't changed his mind about the car. It was the same one he'd seen before.

He half expected to see it parked in the lot beside the roadside cafe when they went out to continue their journey, but it wasn't there. And, as the hours and the miles rolled by, he saw no sign of the older vehicle. He was beginning to believe that his uncle was right. Still, the thought continued to nag at him. It was more than a coincidence. It had to be.

The sun lost its tenuous grasp on the horizon and was slipping out of sight behind the mountains when Mack directed the Texas rancher to turn off the main highway to his village. His excitement was beginning to build the closer they got to the place where he was born.

"Looks as though it's a steep climb," Clarence observed to no one in particular.

"Sí, it is steep, all right, and the road isn't too good. But we will be there before long."

They had been winding tortuously along the side of the steep tree-choked mountain for half an hour or more when they came to a place where a big tree lay across the road.

Clarence braked to a stop. "What's this?" he exclaimed. "It looks as though a tree has blown down."

Mack Flores' eyes widened with terror.

"No, Señor Roper!" he exclaimed, his voice taking on a heavy Spanish accent. "It is not the wind! It is *bandidos!*"

CHAPTER 5

A SINISTER PLAN

For the space of two or three seconds, Clarence remained motionless, frozen at the wheel by Mack Flores' desperate cry.

"Go, Mr. Roper!" the boy shouted. "Go quick! Before they come!"

As though they came in on cue, at that instant two dark figures materialized out of the brush near the side of the road.

Clarence slammed the car into gear and jammed the accelerator against the floorboards. The powerful vehicle lurched forward. He jerked the car expertly to the right, crashing into the small end branches at the top of the fallen tree. There were horrible scratching sounds as branches broke off and clawed at the shining metal. Momentarily the driver's vision was blotted. The wheels bumped over the tree trunk, teetered on the cliff, and came back onto the rough, narrow road.

"Whew!" Clarence exclaimed, involuntarily easing off on the accelerator.

"Keep going, Uncle Clarence!" Doug cried. "Don't stop now, whatever you do!"

"Don't worry! I'm not about to stop until we get to the village!"

* * *

Standing on the edge of the road where he and his companion had been hiding, Red Sanford spun on his heel.

"Now see what you went and done, Juan!" he cried, his face livid with rage.

"Me? What did I do? I wasn't driving the car. I didn't get him over the tree!"

"No, but you picked out such a little tree that they were able to drive over it! Now they got away, and it was all your fault."

Juan faced him blandly. "You could have used my machete, amigo," he said without anger, "and cut down any tree you wanted to. I would have loaned you the machete, señor."

Red swore savagely. "I don't know why I ever teamed up with you. What is the deal, Gonzales? Do I have to do all the thinking and the work, too?"

A smile played with the corners of his friend's mouth. "You no do so good in the thinking department yet, Señor Red. We have not so many pesos now as we have when you start thinking. How about that?"

"Shut up or I'll break you in two!" The American's scowl deepened. "I'm the one who found the wealthy oil man, ain't I? I'm the one who got the man in the motel to talk to the Mexican kid and find out where they were going so we could get here ahead of them, ain't I?"

"Sí."

"Then lay off that kind of talk. I ain't goin' to put up with much more of it."

It was obvious that Sanford's threats did not disturb Juan Gonzales. He had been hearing them ever since they broke away from the prison together, and nothing had come of them yet. Sanford did not frighten him.

"But we still have not as many pesos as we have before," he persisted. "All of your thinking has done nothing for us yet, Señor Red."

Red drew back his fist menacingly, as though hoping for some sign of fear in his companion. But Juan did not flinch.

"Just keep your shirt on and we will have. I promised you that, and I'm going to deliver. But you've got to give me a chance. Big deals like this take time."

Juan grew more serious. "Just what do we do now?" he wanted to know. "How are we going to get so many pesos we can't count them all?"

His companion hesitated. "I wasn't goin' to tell you right yet, but I guess I'm goin' to have to if I'm goin' to keep that big mouth of yours shut." He looked around, the way a man would if he wanted to make sure that he wasn't being overheard.

"You don't have to be so careful about talking out here," Gonzales told him. "There is no one closer to us than that village, and it is on the other side of the mountain."

"We can't be too careful, but I don't suppose you ever thought of that." He lowered his voice. "That oil man's got a kid."

Gonzales laughed. "I suppose you are thinking that you tell me something I don't know. He has three kids and the Mexican boy, too."

"But you don't know what I've got in mind for one of those stupid kids, do you? We're goin' to kidnap him and hold him for ransom."

Juan Gonzales' eyes gleamed. "No!" he cried aloud.

"That's right. We'll snatch him from under the old man's nose and take him up in the hills. We won't let him go until that millionaire dad of his pays us a pile of money."

Juan thought about that. Until this very moment he hadn't really taken Red Sanford seriously. Oh, he knew that his friend had stolen a lot of stuff on the other side of the border and had been in jail in both Mexico and the States, but he thought all of this business about the wealthy American had been talk, especially since they weren't able to stop him and rob him by cutting down the tree and pulling it across the road. He hadn't figured that Sanford had any plan in mind.

"We won't hurt him, will we?" he asked. "The kid, I mean."

"Oh, no, we won't hurt him. We'll just take him and keep him for a few days, that's all. Now, what do you think of that for an idea?"

Juan licked his lips. The more he thought about it, the more excited he became over the idea. There wasn't any doubt that the rich Americano liked his sons. If he hadn't, he wouldn't have brought them along on this trip to Mexico. He just might think enough of one that he would give them two or three hundred pesos to get him back.

"How much we ask for?"

A grin teased the corners of Red's mouth. "How much do you think?"

Juan shrugged. "If I knew, señor, I would not ask you."

Red leaned forward triumphantly. "What would you think about asking a bushel of pesos?"

Gonzales cried out in surprise. "A bushel of pesos?"

"Or maybe even two bushels!"

"You make the joke."

"That's right, Gonzales, I'm just joking. I really figure on asking five million pesos!"

Juan's breath slammed out of him, and his mouth sagged open. "There aren't so many pesos in all of Mexico!"

"That's all you know about it. If we had a little

more time, we could get ten million pesos, maybe, but we don't want to be greedy."

Gonzales picked up a twig and began breaking pieces off thoughtfully. Five million pesos! He and Sanford would be rich men! It had been a lucky day when he had gotten caught stealing the cow and had been thrown in jail in Matamoras. That was where he had met Red Sanford. And now Sanford was going to make him rich.

* * *

Mr. Roper drove faster than usual the rest of the way to The Congregation of the Bulls. The boys kept a sharp lookout for some sign of the bandits, but there was nothing to indicate that they were anywhere around.

"I don't think they'll bother us anymore," Mack said, his voice revealing his relief. "I think we got away from them okay."

"I'm beginning to agree with you." The rancher sighed deeply. "But for a minute or so I thought they had caught us for sure."

They continued to jounce over the rough mountain road. Doug Davis was staring uneasily into the brush on their right, and Phil and Del were doing the same on the other side. Although they saw nothing to indicate there were any bandits still in the area, Doug was uneasy.

Ever since they had seen that old car following

them in Victoria, strange things had been happening – things he had been doing a great deal of thinking about. He didn't know how the men in the old car could figure in with the tree that had been felled across the mountain road. It seemed silly even to think there was any connection. But, somehow, he had the uneasy feeling that this all tied in with the strangers in some way. The fact that he couldn't imagine how it all went together didn't help him to feel any more at ease.

Those men had gone by when Mr. Roper and the boys were in the cafe eating lunch, so conceivably they could have been the ones to cut down the tree and try to stop them. But it hadn't happened on the highway. It had happened on an obscure little mountain trail. How could they have known that the car was going to turn off on that particular road? And how had they known that the car would be coming along at that particular time?

Those were elements Doug couldn't reason out. The more he thought about them the more bewildered he became. They didn't make sense at all.

Clarence was also thinking about the bandits who had tried to stop them. He, too, considered the two men that the boys had claimed were following them. He had also dismissed the idea as preposterous that they could have followed them this far without being seen.

He glanced in Mack's direction. "Are there a lot of bandits in these mountains, Mack?" he asked.

The Mexican boy shook his head. "No, Mr. Roper, there are few *bandidos* here. Everybody is so poor–" He shrugged expressively. "There is nothing around our village to steal."

The Texas rancher nodded grimly. That was the way he had figured it. That and the fact that the people were hard working and industrious and honest, even though they had very little.

"There are a lot of things about that tree being across the road that disturb me," he went on. "It seems mighty strange to me that they would just happen to put that roadblock up before we came along. It's almost as though they knew that we were coming." He paused significantly. "Do you suppose they did?"

Mack Flores' frown drove away the smile from his face. "I do not see how they could know we were coming, Mr. Roper, but maybe they did." His gaze searched Clarence's. "I did not write anyone in our village that we were coming, so no one in The Congregation of the Bulls knows about our visit. It couldn't have been anyone from our village."

Phil spoke up. "Maybe they had a lookout on the trail and spotted us. It wouldn't take much time to cut down a tree and drop it across the road."

"It wouldn't, at that." Clarence tightened his grip on the wheel. "But from the looks of this road there hasn't been another car over it in the last week. Why would bandits wait on a road like this that is only used a few times a month? It doesn't make sense to me."

The boys lapsed into silence. There was no figuring out why it happened. They could only be glad that things had worked out the way they had.

It was half an hour later when they neared Mack's village. It was like a dozen others they had traveled through since reaching Mexico – a handful of rickety stick and mud houses scattered carelessly along the steep slope. The narrow, rutted road twisted past a crude corral where two or three bony, long horned cattle munched wearily on a handful of cane stalks. It turned to skirt an enclosure that held a half-grown litter of pigs and came to a small square that represented the center of The Congregation of the Bulls. There was a store on the east side and one on the north – little buildings as ramshackle and dilapidated as the houses. Only the inevitable signs advertising a popular American soft drink designated them as places of merchandise.

"Well, here we are!" Mack exclaimed proudly. "This is *my* village!"

"Where do we go now, Mack?" Clarence took his gaze off the road long enough to glance at the youthful Mexican at his side.

"Stop here." He didn't want to appear excited, but he was. His cheeks were flushed and anticipation flamed high in his eyes.

There had been half a dozen boys and girls playing in the square as they drove up, but as soon as the vehicle stopped, they disappeared as if some magic carpet had swooped down, gathered them up, and whisked them all away. There were no men in view, either. That was somewhat surprising to Clarence. He had thought someone would come out to meet them.

Slowly Mack got out of the car, his keen young eyes darting this direction and that. After a long minute a ragged figure materialized from the shadows.

"Mack!" a high pitched young voice cried.

He spun on his heel. "Eduardo!" He dashed forward. "Eduardo!"

The other boy ran to meet him halfway.

By this time others began to appear. They came out of dark corners and spots of opaque blackness that seemed incapable of holding one of the many mangy dogs that inhabited the village, let alone a boy or a girl. In an instant Mack was surrounded by talking, laughing youngsters.

Del and Doug Davis listened, numbed by the torrential cloudburst of Spanish. They thought they could understand the language fairly well; in fact, they would have classified themselves as being good at the language. But not when it came in a flood like this.

It wasn't long until curious adults began to come out of their homes to see what was going on.

"It is Mack!" Eduardo shrilled above the others. "It's Mack Flores! He's come home!"

Laughing, Phil turned to his cousins. "They're sure glad to see him, aren't they?"

"You can say that again," they answered.

Mack's aunts came up to him first among the adults. They looked so much like the boy's mother that both Del and Doug were amazed. They wanted to know how she was and how the little ones were doing. Were they all well? Did they have enough to eat? Where did they live?

Mack answered the questions as best he could. They seemed pleased with what he was able to tell them.

At last there was a pause.

His father's brother approached, and Mack greeted him warmly. "It is so good to see you Uncle Felipe."

"It is good to see you, Mack. But why do you come back to our poor village?" Felipe Flores' black eyes were piercing. "If everything is so well for you and your mother and the little ones in Texas, why do you come back here?"

Mack eyed him uneasily. The color drained slowly from his cheeks, and he began to tremble inside. He had forgotten all about his Uncle Felipe Flores when he and Mr. Roper were talking about coming down to The Congregation of the Bulls to tell the people about Jesus Christ. He had forgotten about his uncle's zeal for the religion of his family and the people of the village.

What would Uncle Felipe do or say when he found out why they had come?

The tip of Mack's tongue appeared between his thin lips.

CHAPTER 6

A FAMILY REUNION

Mack Flores cleared his throat uneasily. He could feel Uncle Felipe's cold, questioning stare boring through him, demanding explanations that would be hard to give. What could he tell him that would not make him so angry? How could he explain why they had come to the village of his birth? What could he tell one with a temper like that of his uncle?

Mack was still fumbling for words, but Uncle Felipe did not wait for him to reply.

"Why you come back here?" His uncle's voice was hard and unreasoning, a taut, hostile voice, delicately honed with suspicion. Even as he spoke, he was looking beyond Mack at Clarence Roper who was standing a few feet away. "Why does this–this Americano bring you to our village from his fine home in America? What does he want from us, Mack? What do we have that he wants?"

"He wants nothing from you, Uncle Felipe," Mack said quickly, as though the very haste with which he denied the charge would carry weight. "I have been wanting to tell you about the Señor Americano who brings me back to The Congregation of the Bulls. He is Clarence Roper."

Felipe's eyes lightened briefly.

"Señor Roper?" he echoed. "The man who gave your mama the cooking job on the rancho? Is he the one who gave you and the little ones a place to stay?"

"Sí." Mack nodded vigorously. "This is Señor Roper. He is our friend."

Felipe Flores had no more questions. He approached Clarence Roper seriously, his hand extended.

"I wish to shake the hand with you, señor." He had been to America several times, working in the beet fields and could speak a certain amount of English. It was broken, to be sure, but they could all understand him easily. "You are our friend," he continued. "What we have in our poor little village is yours." He gestured widely.

Mr. Roper's smile was infectious and brought a smile to the other man's lips.

"Gracias, Señor Flores. Thank you. We have our own tents and our own food, so we won't be a burden to anyone, but we are glad for your kindness. Thank you."

"My friends call me Felipe."

"Felipe, it is."

They shook hands once more.

The others of the village had clustered about, watching and listening in silence as Felipe Flores questioned his nephew and talked with the tall Americano. Now that they saw that Felipe was accepting the stranger without question, they did the same, moving forward quietly and shaking hands with him. It was obvious to Clarence and the boys that Felipe was a leader in the village. When he gave his approval to an individual, the others accepted that person, without question, as a friend.

While the boys and the curious villagers gathered and listened, Felipe continued to talk with Mr. Roper. He had many questions to ask. After all, he had a responsibility to his dead brother to find out how his family was doing. He wanted to know about his sister-in-law and her fatherless brood. Were they well? Did they like it on the other side of the border? Was their food enough for them to eat? Did they have clothes enough to keep warm when the north wind rattled the windows and stole in around the door? Were they happy?

Clarence replied as honestly as he was able. The kids, he said, were as happy as though they were living here in the village. His sister-in-law was happy most of the time, but there were days when her eyes were sad and her heart heavy for her own people. Felipe nodded, indicating that he understood.

"Sí, I know how she longs for our village and her

sisters and their children. I am feeling the same way when I am working in the beet fields across the border. There are times when I am happy, but there are other times, especially when the work is done and we have only to sit on the steps and think about our wives and our children at home. Then I hurt so bad I think maybe something break inside." He tapped his chest significantly.

While the men and Mack were talking, Del and Doug and their cousin, Phil, walked over to one of the small stores to explore. Three or four smaller children followed them from some distance, watching what they did with keen interest.

"It makes me feel sort of funny having them tag along behind us and stare at us the way they're doing now," Phil said softly.

The Davis boys nodded. "That was the way it was when our folks first went to Guatemala before we were born. I can remember hearing Mom and Dad tell about it. They said the people had never seen anyone with such white skin before. Maybe that's the deal here. We probably look different than the people they're used to."

"They're sure nice and friendly," Del added. "At first I thought that uncle of Mack's was going to take us apart, but when he found out who your dad was, he acted as though he was his best friend."

"That's one thing that's great about the Mexican

people. If you are friendly and treat them right, they'll be the same to you," Phil said.

Del snickered.

"Now what's so funny?" his brother asked.

"I was thinking about that Juan Gonzales who was following us. Now he was one of those friendly ones, it was easy to see."

"He wasn't as bad as the American who was with him," Phil put in. "You've got to admit that."

"You may have a point there. But neither one of them would win any prizes for being agreeable."

"You can say that again." He stopped quickly. "I just thought of something! Do you think those two had anything to do with that tree being across the road this afternoon?"

Phil shook his head. "Not a chance. How would they have known where we left the main road?"

"They could have been watching."

"That would have put them behind us."

"Maybe so." Del knew reason was on Phil's side, but he couldn't help feeling the way he did. He took two or three steps to one side, staring intently up the mountain slope in the growing darkness.

"What're you looking at?" Scorn lightly edged Doug's voice.

"I was wondering about those two oddballs," Del went on. "I don't know how they could have found out where we were going and which road we would turn on, but you've got to admit that trick sounds about like them."

Phil turned back to the car. "Those guys didn't have anything to do with that fallen tree," Phil said decisively. "I'd bet on it. And I don't think we'll ever see them again."

* * *

At that very moment in the jungle not far from the isolated village where Mack Flores was born, Sanford was pacing uneasily back and forth in front of their old car.

"You're sure you covered our car good, Juan?" he asked, his temper as short as his hair. "You've fouled up everything else you've done."

"How many times I have to tell you it's okay?"

"It had better be. We'll be needing it bad when the time comes."

Disgust edged Juan's usually placid voice. "You could cover it yourself, Señor Red, if you do not trust me."

"I trust you all right." He allowed the anger to seep from the words. "But I don't want anything to happen to our car before we're ready to snatch the kid, that's all. If somebody stumbles onto it, the whole deal blows up. Like that!" He snapped his fingers.

"Nobody see the car, I tell you," Juan assured him. "When I hide her, I hide her good, amigo."

Red sat down wearily and leaned against a tree. "I'm tired, Gonzales."

"You tired? I am the one who should be tired. I cut down the tree and I cut branches and cover up our car. If anybody is tired it should be me."

"The thinking is the hard work. But I don't suppose you would know about that."

Juan went over and stood before him. "When do we steal the kid so we get all those pesos? Tonight?"

Red shook his head. "No, we're not goin' to steal him tonight. We've got to work out our plan first. We've got to plan!"

"Sí, señor," Gonzales said, his dark eyes narrowing ominously. "You plan. I work. That is the way it goes. But this I tell you right now. I do not steal the kid alone. You go with me, or it is off! Finished! You understand?"

"Okay, okay!" He tried to control his disgust with his companion. "To tell you the truth, Juan, I wouldn't trust you to pull off a job like this alone. I'm goin' to be in on it to see that it goes right. Don't you forget it."

Gonzales nodded. "Sí, Señor Red." It should have been obvious he was taunting his companion, needling him about his own lack of courage. "That suits me just fine. If you want to do it alone, I can wait for you up here, okay? I think maybe that is one good idea. You go down and steal the kid. I go after the pesos. Okay?"

Red swore. "Shut up and let me think!"

Juan grinned. "Some time it seems to me you not do so good in thinking, Señor Red. How it be if I help you do that, too?"

Sanford's scowl deepened. He didn't like to have Gonzales joke about anything so serious as the kidnapping they were planning. A man had to work things out in his head, that was all there was to it. He had to get all the details straight if he was going to make so many pesos in so short a time. If that stupid Juan wasn't careful, Red would run off and leave him when he pulled the job and the rich Texan paid off to get his son back. He wouldn't need him anymore, then. And, Red told himself, if he did cut Gonzales out of the money, it would serve him right. Gonzales ought to treat him with the proper respect.

* * *

Clarence Roper finished visiting with Felipe, and the slight, dark-skinned Mexican, who looked very much like Mack, went back to his home. Only after he was gone did the Texas rancher remember that they hadn't yet found a place to set up camp. He turned to Mack.

"We've got to get our tent pitched and fix something to eat so we can get to bed, Mack. Would you go and ask your uncle where he'd like to have us locate?"

"Sí." Mack scampered off. Almost before everyone expected him to return, he was back.

"Uncle Felipe says there is a good place over by the old church to put up our tents. It is high ground if it should rain."

Clarence drove the car up to the ramshackle church building with broken windows and sagging doors.

"It looks as though it's been a long time since church services have been held here," he observed.

"I didn't hear anyone say how long it is since there was church here," Mack answered. I asked my mama about it once and she said the people were too poor. Nobody came to church and after a while there was no one to preach."

The corners of Mr. Roper's mouth were taut and set grimly. "That's one of the reasons we wanted to come here and talk to the people. Everybody should have a chance to hear about Jesus Christ."

"Sí." Mack beamed. "Sí. That is why we came."

Everybody in the party had a job, and they all set to work efficiently. Clarence got the gasoline stove, lit it, and started to fix supper while the boys set up camp. Doug and Del got the tent off the rack on top of the car and pitched it expertly, while Phil and Mack set up the other tent and got out the sleeping bags.

They were all so tired that night that they went to bed as soon as they finished supper and did the dishes. Phil was the last to crawl into his sleeping bag.

"I'm sure glad Dad had us make a ditch around

the tents tonight," he said. "I think it's going to rain before morning."

Doug and Del scoffed at his prediction. "What do you mean rain? There's not a cloud in the sky."

"That's what you think. Take a look outside now. It's as dark as pitch and there's lightning in the west."

Del rolled over on his side. "Know what I'm going to do about it? I'm going to let it rain."

Phil's prediction came true before midnight. With a rush the rain and wind swept down from the mountain to swallow the little village. The Davis boys stirred sleepily, only half awakened by the roaring rain and wind. Phil raised on one elbow, listening.

"Hear that?" he echoed. "What'd I tell you? It's raining!" A tone of triumph crept into his voice.

Doug scrunched farther into his sleeping bag and covered his head. "Big deal!"

"And you guys were trying to tell me I didn't know what I was talking about."

"As long as the tent stays over us, I couldn't care less," Del told him.

For several minutes they lay in the tent listening to the wild ravings of the storm. They found it impossible to sleep while it was at its height, but after an hour or so the wind and rain both began to slacken, and they closed their eyes once again. Sleep came instantly and the next thing they knew it was morning.

Mack was the first one up. "Hey, you guys! What're you going to do, stay in bed all day?"

"Go 'way," Phil muttered. "You're makin' too much noise."

"Get out of there. The sun's shining bright!"

He pushed the tent flap aside and stepped out into the brilliant subtropical sunlight. He really didn't care if the others didn't get up right away. He was going down and find some of his old friends.

Mack hurried down the path fifty or sixty yards before a strange uneasiness swept over him. By this time almost everyone in the village should be up.

But they weren't! There was no one in the square or on the paths. He didn't even see anyone in front of the mud huts. He stopped suddenly.

Where was everybody? It was as though they had all been swept away by some strange magic!

CHAPTER 7

DANGER COMES CLOSER

Numbly, Mack stared around the silent mountain village. A few goats were grazing on the steep slope to his right, and a dog was foraging for his breakfast at the back of one of the huts where a bucket of garbage had been thrown. But that was all.

Something strange was going on in The Congregation of the Bulls – something he did not understand. In all the years he had lived there, he had never seen the settlement so quiet, so void of life this hour of the morning. He was still motionless, transfixed by the heavy, oppressive silence, when Phil and Del came up beside him.

"What's the big idea of waking us up so early?" Phil wanted to know. "Take a look. No one else is even out of bed yet."

Mack pivoted to face them. "That's just it! There

ought to be a lot of people awake now. Everyone here gets up early."

"What do you think's wrong?" Del asked.

"Let's don't just stand here!" Phil Roper hurried down the trail ahead of his companions. "Let's get over to your uncle's and see what the deal is."

"That's a good idea." Mack was almost running by the time they reached his uncle's house. He was calling out to them when they were still some distance away. "Uncle Felipe! Uncle Felipe!"

At the first sound of his voice his aunt appeared in the doorway. She squealed with delight when she saw him and rushed out to meet him.

"Mack!" She threw her arms about him. "Oh, Mack! It is so good to see you!" She was thrilled for the chance to see Mack away from his uncle, who dominated every conversation.

He struggled, briefly, to free himself from the fervor of her embrace. It was good to see her and all of that, but he didn't know what the guys would think, seeing the way she greeted him. At last she freed him, tears moistening her cheeks.

"Your Uncle Felipe tells us all about you last night. We are all so glad you come back to see us!"

She had a hundred questions to ask him, questions that would not wait for the matter he wanted to ask about. They tumbled out in Spanish as rapidly as the flood waters were flowing in the little creek near the village. He tried to answer her, but each reply triggered another question until they both were breathless. It was some time before the torrent of words stopped long enough for him to ask a question of his own.

"Where is Uncle Felipe?" he demanded at last. "And where is everybody else?" He gestured widely with his thin brown arm. "I see nobody in the village."

Her eyes danced. "Don't you know?" she asked. "It rained last night."

"I know it rained." In spite of his efforts to hold it back, his irritation showed through. "But what does that have to do with it?"

"You would not know, of course." Her laughter trilled with the happiness he used to hear in his mother's voice before papa died. "Good days have come to the village since you were last here, Mack."

"But what does that have to do with the rain?"

"Everything. After every rain the men and the boys and even the girls who are big enough go up to the ancient burial grounds to look for treasure. The rains wash valuable things from the ground – an old pot for holding water or food, some dishes, some little figures, and clay in the shape of heads."

Mack nodded. He knew about the burial grounds. Sometimes after a rain, he and Eduardo used to go up to the burial mound themselves to look for such things. And, if anything interested them, they brought it home and kept it until their mamas tired of seeing it and threw it out. Only nobody called them treasures in those days. They were worth nothing.

"But what do you do with them?" he wanted to know. "How do they bring good days to the village?"

"An Americano comes in a big car. He looks at them and sometimes he gives us a peso for a head, four pesos for a bowl if it isn't cracked, and things like that. After every rain all the people in the village, except the women like me with babies too small to take, hurry to the place of the dead and look for treasure."

Mack listened curiously while his aunt talked about the treasures that came from the place of the dead. He didn't understand much about it, and he didn't think she did, either, from the way she answered his questions. She didn't know why the pieces of clay were so valuable. She didn't know what the Americano did with them.

"We don't ask him," she said. "We think maybe he will change his mind and stop buying them if we let him know how foolish we think he is."

With that she changed the subject. Mack was anxious to be away, and he knew his companions were, too, but there was no chance for them to leave yet. He had to stay a while longer and visit with her. Del, who understood most of what she had said about the treasures from the burial grounds, relayed the information to his cousin, Phil.

"That's a good joke on us," Phil said, grinning. "And we thought everyone had been washed down the mountain in the rain when they're just up on the hill looking for old pieces of clay."

Del was curious. "What would an American do with stuff like that?" he wanted to know.

"Search me." Phil shrugged expressively. "But whatever he does with it, I'll bet he's making plenty of money out of it. If he wasn't, he wouldn't be driving all the way down here to buy up old junk."

"You're right about that. He sure wouldn't do it because he feels sorry for the people."

When they got back to the campsite, Mr. Roper was very curious about the ancient pottery pieces the American was buying.

"I'm like you, Phil. He must have a scheme worked out where he can make a lot of money on that stuff, or he wouldn't be doing it."

His son ran his hand across his forehead as though to smooth out the deepening wrinkles his dad's remark brought. "But what would he do with them? That's what we couldn't figure out. Who would want a pile of junk like that?"

The Texas rancher was staring curiously in the direction of the ancient burial grounds. "I don't know for sure, but I can tell you this much, I'm going to try to find out before he comes back again."

The boys and Mr. Roper discussed the matter as they fixed breakfast and finally decided to go up to the burial mounds themselves as soon as they finished eating. But before they had the dishes done, the first stragglers of the villagers came shuffling down the trail, Felipe among them. He came over to see them.

"It was not so good this morning," he said, setting his cloth sack on the hood of the car and taking the pieces of old pottery from inside. He had two or three small bowls that were perfect, one bowl had a chip broken out of it, and a couple of figures with a leg or an arm broken off. "I only get a few pieces. Maybe the señor give me something for them."

"This isn't really any business of mine, Felipe," Clarence said, "but have you ever tried to find out what the American does with the artifacts you sell to him?"

He shook his head.

"Do you have any idea who he sells them to or how much he gets out of them?"

"No, señor. He says they aren't worth much, that he only buys them to help us out." He paused. "Maybe he does not tell us the truth, but the pesos we get for them have been a help to our village. It is good for us that he comes."

"I'm sure that's right, but wouldn't it be better if you could get five or ten or twenty times as much?"

"Sí, it would be better." But the tone of his voice revealed that he did not understand.

"I've been doing a lot of thinking about this ever since the boys came back from your place and told me what you and the other villagers were doing this morning. How about you and I taking a few of the better pieces and driving down to Monte? We can soon find out what they're worth."

Felipe had to consider that. It had never occurred to him that they might be able to sell the artifacts themselves and get more money for them than what the Americano was giving them.

"Do you think it would be all right, señor?"

"It's the only thing to do, Felipe. Maybe the man who buys these things *is* giving you what they're actually worth. Maybe he is not giving you enough. If we go down to Monte, we can find someone who can tell us."

"It is good, Señor Roper." There was a tone of respect and approval in his voice, as though he too trusted Clarence, even as Mack and his family did. "I go and tell my wife that we are going. Then I am ready."

Clarence asked the boys if they wanted to ride along. At first they hesitated, as though undecided, but at the last minute they made up their minds.

"I think we'd rather stay around here and see things, Dad," Phil said.

"Okay, but don't get into trouble. Y'hear?"

"You know we wouldn't get into trouble."

"I know you guys. That's why I warned you."

* * *

Up on the mountain Juan Gonzales and Red Sanford were just drying out after the soaking rain. Red was miserable, and so was his temper.

"I don't know why I let you talk me into leaving the car, Gonzales," he complained. "If we'd stayed there, at least we'd have been dry."

"What are you saying? I did not talk you into leaving the car. You are the one who says we have to get closer to the village. We have to find out where the Señor Millionaire and his sons stay."

"All right! All right!" Red pushed his way through the trees and thick undergrowth. "Forget it!"

Silently his Mexican companion followed him. It was not Juan's nature to argue with anyone, even a person like Sanford. It was not that he was afraid of him. Actually, Red was afraid of Gonzales in spite of the blustering he did. Juan half sensed that, too, and it amused him, although he said nothing about it.

They had pushed their way through the tangled jungle for fifteen or twenty minutes when suddenly they were close enough to see The Congregation of the Bulls. Red Sanford sucked in his breath in a quick gasp.

"There it is, Gonzales!" Greed choked his voice. "There's our five million pesos! Think of that!"

"Sí."

"If you just hold up your end of the bargain and don't mess up the deal, we'll have everything going our way. Five million pesos!"

"Sí," Gonzales repeated, licking his lips once more. He could not imagine what five million pesos was. One sack full? Two sacks full? A truckload, maybe?

The more he thought about it, the more sure he was that a truckload of pesos would be about right. Five million pesos was so many that *nobody* could count them. When he thought of it that way, he hoped the Americano paid off in dollars. They would be so much easier to carry.

But what would he do with American dollars? The people in his own village wouldn't even know what they were. No, he wanted his share in pesos – big, round, heavy pesos that would jingle in his pocket when he walked. He would get a whole string of bur-ros to carry them if he had to.

The mental picture of himself leading a line of burros along the highway, one behind the other, brought a smile to his face. What would the people think when they saw him?

The smile faded. He wished there was some other way of getting the money other than stealing some man's son. He knew how he had felt stealing that cow. It had not been a good feeling, and he was almost glad when they caught him. But it was like Señor Red said, the Señor Millionaire had so much money that he would never miss it, maybe. He would get the note and send someone to the bank to get it – pronto. And if he did not have enough, he would have only to wait a day or two until his so-many oil wells pumped it out of the ground for him.

Juan turned to his associate, and for the first time in almost an hour he spoke aloud. "When we do it, señor?"

Red lowered his voice subconsciously, although they both knew there was no one within hearing distance.

"Tonight, if everything works out. We find where the boys stay, and we sneak down and grab one before he knows what's happened to him!"

Juan Gonzales nodded. It sounded so easy when Red talked about it. He tried to keep thinking about what his companion said and not to the quiet urging of his own thoughts.

"But right now, Gonzales, we've got to go down close enough to the village to find out as much as we can. We've got to *know* where that boy's going to be tonight!"

The closer the two men got to the mountain settlement, the more stealthily they moved. There was always a chance, Gonzales knew, that a couple of venturesome boys would be prowling through the jungle and come upon them. And if that happened, he reasoned, everything would be lost!

They were not far from the outer rim of the jungle when Sanford stopped quickly, crouching to peer through the brush.

"What is it?" Juan's whisper was hoarse.

"Shh-h-h!" Red held a finger to his mouth in warning.

An instant later Roper started the engine of the car and turned around to head back down the road. Juan Gonzales groaned aloud.

"They are leaving! Now we cannot get our five million pesos!"

CHAPTER 8

FEAR OF ANGRY SPIRITS

As the car slowly negotiated the turn and picked up speed until it jounced out of view, Juan Gonzales groaned a second time, even louder than before.

"There they go!" New agony etched itself in his voice, as though the pain was almost more than he could bear. "Now we will never get all of those pesos from the Señor Millionaire!"

He had scarcely finished speaking when Red Sanford's bony fingers clamped on his forearm and tightened until he winced. "What's the matter with you, stupid?" the American demanded. "If you keep talking so loud, they'll be sure to hear you!"

Gonzales jerked to face him, disgust in every move. "What difference does that make now? The Americano is gone and so is our money!"

"I just happen to want to stay out of jail, for one thing. And for another–"

The words clogged his throat. At that moment, Del and Doug Davis stepped from behind the dilapidated church in plain view of Juan and Red's hiding place. Both men saw the American boys at the same time.

"There they are!" Red's whispering voice broke with emotion. "Are we ever in luck! They haven't gone after all!"

Once Gonzales recovered from the initial shock, his expansive smile lit his face.

"Sí, señor! Maybe we get one more chance to get all that money, no?"

Sanford trembled with excitement. "We'll get one more chance, I'll promise you that. And what's more, we're going to get more money from that rich Texan than you ever saw at one time."

Gonzales did not answer him. Sanford probably didn't know it, but Juan had never in all his life seen so many as one thousand pesos. Even if he got more than he had ever seen, it might not be so much. But it would be more than he had now. The prospect brought a glow to his cheeks.

Red breathed deeply. "We're going to be rich, Gonzales!" he repeated. "Rich! Now, what do you think of that?"

A grin split the squat little Mexican's face. "That is the kind of talk I like to hear, Señor Red. It makes me glad that we are friends."

The American nodded. "We'll kidnap the boy and get the ransom money pronto, okay?"

"Sí."

"We'll get it, but we've got to work out our plans, so we know exactly what to do." He was cautious now. He had never planned anything this big before. The other times he stole, he had snitched an envelope from a mailbox or broken into a store for cigarettes and liquor to sell. This was different. He had to have all the details in mind. "It takes brains to pull off a job like this." He tapped his forehead with his index finger. "It takes brains. Understand?"

"Sí, señor." He was about to tease the Americano by telling him that this was why he wanted to do all the planning himself or at least to get in on it. But he did not. He knew he did not have any idea of carrying out what his friend planned. It was better now to remain quiet and do what he was told. There would be time enough for joking after he had the sixteen burro-loads of pesos. With some reasoning which he did not entirely understand himself, he had decided that his share of the five million pesos would be enough load for sixteen burros.

* * *

Clarence and Mack's uncle, Felipe Flores, had not been gone from The Congregation of the Bulls more than a few minutes when Mack's old friends began to move closer to the tent. They came shyly, scuffing their feet in the rain-soaked grass, their heads lowered with their accepted form of politeness. Mack bounded over to them excitedly, talking with first one and then another. He hadn't realized he would be so glad to get home.

After a time the boys learned that Doug and Del spoke Spanish with some degree of fluency and that Phil could do fairly well if they spoke slowly and distinctly. They seemed to enjoy talking with the boys whose skin was so much lighter than theirs.

Mack was the first to mention the Lord Jesus Christ and what He had done for him. He turned to the boy who had been his best friend when he still lived in the village. "Did I tell you what happened to me since we went to Texas, Eduardo?" he asked.

His friend shook his head. He was interested. They all wanted to hear about the land north of the Rio Grande River where Mack and his mother and the little ones were now living.

"I am a Christian now," he said. "I am a follower of the One called Jesus." He went on to explain how happy he was since he had turned from the old ways. He was no longer afraid of the spirits that so many of the villagers feared and worshiped.

"Do not talk so bold, Mack!" The color leaked from Eduardo's cheeks and his lips trembled slightly. "The spirits will not like it. There's no knowing what they will do to you if they get mad at what you say!"

He smiled at his friend's superstition, but his smile was far from reassuring to Eduardo and the others. Fear lurked in their eyes, and they glanced about uneasily, expecting the spirits to manifest themselves at any instant.

"I am no longer afraid of the spirits," Mack said calmly. "They can do nothing to me."

"You don't *know* what they can do. They can spirit you out of your bed at night and whisk you away so no one will ever see you again."

"Or they may make something to fall on you when you are out in the jungle."

Mack wanted to tell them more of Jesus, but they would not allow him to. He was silent for a moment.

"Why do you wait until after a rain to go and look for pieces of pottery and little figures?" he asked them. He knew the answer to his question, but he wanted to hear them tell him.

Eduardo spoke quickly. "If the rain washes them out of the place of the dead, the spirits do not care. So, we can go and pick them up."

"You could get more if you dug them."

He stared in horror. "We wouldn't dare! The spirits would–" He stopped, afraid even to say what the spirits might do if anyone should dare such a terrible act.

"You know what we're going to do?" Mack said firmly. "We're going to take shovels and go up there and dig. We'll get a lot of dishes and figures and make much money."

The eyes of the other Mexican boys widened.

"No!" Eduardo's voice was a harsh whisper. "No! Don't do that thing!"

"We're not afraid," Mack repeated. "And we want to show you that we're not afraid. We're going to prove to you that the spirits can't hurt us."

Eduardo seemed to sense that Mack could not be dissuaded, but he turned hopefully to Phil.

"The spirits be *mucho* angry if you do this thing! They take terrible vengeance on you!"

Phil's smile was as confident as Mack's. "We're not afraid of the spirits."

Eduardo gave up on him and directed his attention to the Davis boys. "You can stop them! Make them change their minds about this terrible thing!"

"We're not afraid, either." They knew how important it was to show the village boys that they were actually unafraid of the spirits. Nothing else would have such an effect on them.

"That's right," Doug added. "In fact, I'd like to go up there right now and get started. How about it?"

The Mexican boys eyed one another questioningly. They were fearful for Mack and his Americano friends, that was true, but they were also excited about the prospect of defying the spirits. They wanted to see what would happen. They were whispering guardedly to one another as Mack borrowed machetes for himself and Phil and the two Davis boys. When they had them, he started resolutely up the path in the direction of the ancient burial mounds.

"Let's go." Mack spoke loudly so all his Mexican friends could know for sure that he was not afraid.

The four of them walked briskly up the trail in the direction of the place of the dead. Fearfully, but so curious that they could not keep from following, a dozen or so ragged village boys tagged after them. Their faces were drawn and their movements tense, but a great excitement gleamed in their black eyes. This was, indeed, something they had never seen before. It was something the old men talked about, darkly, in the hush of the night. There was someone, a long while ago, who had angered the spirits, and he was never seen again.

Now they were going to see the spirits defied right in their own village!

There was no doubt in their minds that something horrible was going to happen. The only question was, in what way were the spirits going to exact their revenge?

It was only a ten or fifteen minute walk up the trail to the burial mounds. Mack had not been there for a long while, but he still knew the way so well it was as though he had made the trip the day before. His features were serious, but the three American boys were enjoying it all a great deal. It was not only great fun, but it was also an opportunity to show everyone in the remote little settlement that they need not fear the spirits that they and their fathers and their father's fathers had been so terrified of.

They reached the burial mounds in a few minutes. The sight of the place sobered the youthful villagers who had been following some distance behind Mack and his American friends. They all stopped uneasily. All, that was, except Eduardo. He dashed forward in one final attempt to stop what was about to happen and grasped Mack by the arm.

"No, Mack!" Fear and desperation mingled in his quavering young voice. "Don't do it! The spirits will be *mucho* angry! They do bad things to you and your friends!"

Mack shook off his hand. "It's like I told you, Eduardo, we're not afraid of the spirits!"

As if to underline their lack of fear, Doug Davis took his machete and began to dig in the rain-softened ground. The Mexican boys were motionless some twenty or thirty paces away, transfixed by the foolhardy thing that was happening.

* * *

In the trees not far away, screened by the thick undergrowth, Sanford and Gonzales crouched tensely, watching what was taking place. The American turned to his companion.

"What're they doing, Juan?" His voice was a thin whisper.

"Something bad!" Gonzales replied under his breath. "*Mucho* bad! The spirits be angry with them and do things to make them sorry!"

Red Sanford studied the situation hurriedly. This was an opportunity he had not counted on, one of those strange happenings that come only once and must be seized before the chance disappears, never to come back again.

"Something very good is going to come out of this for you and me, Gonzales," he whispered.

"What do you mean?"

"We are going to kidnap ourselves a boy, that's what I mean!"

Gonzales gasped. "You–you mean we are going to do it now? Today?"

"That's right. We'll never get another chance that's any better than this one."

That news was staggering to Juan Gonzales. He had wanted to go ahead with the kidnapping. Never in his life would he get another chance to have sixteen burro-loads of pesos, pesos the rich Señor Millionaire would never miss. But now that the time was there, he was beginning to change his mind. Kidnapping a boy did not seem good to him. He glanced at Sanford. But how could he say anything about it now to the Americano who was with him and who was taking him in on the deal?

Grimly he pushed his fears away. "Sí. What do we do now?"

"Follow me and be ready to do what I tell you," Red whispered tautly.

They crept stealthily through the thick bush until they reached a place not far from where Doug Davis was working. Red waited tensely until the others moved a short distance away. Then he pushed the branches partially aside.

"Psst!" He spoke just loud enough for Doug to hear him.

The boy's head snapped erect, and he looked around.

"Over here!" Red called. "Quick!"

"Who are you? What do you want?"

Red was careful not to allow enough of himself to be seen so Doug could recognize him.

"Don't get the others excited, but come over here."

Curiously he did as he was told. When he was within arm's reach of Red, the man grabbed him and jerked him into the jungle. Doug struggled valiantly.

"Help! Help!"

Gonzales clamped a muscular hand over his mouth to shut off his screaming.

CHAPTER 9

KIDNAPPED!

Doug Davis struggled hard to free himself from the clutches of Red and his Mexican companion. Had he only been battling one of them he might have succeeded, but the two men were too much for him. The harder he struggled the tighter Red clamped his powerful arms around him and the tighter Gonzales held his hand over Doug's mouth.

He could feel the strength going out of his body. Still battling desperately he managed to part his teeth enough to get hold of Juan's finger and bite it savagely.

"Ouch!" The squat Mexican jerked his finger out of the boy's mouth.

"Help!" Doug shrilled, his piercing cry echoing through the jungle. "Help!"

"Juan!" Sanford was terrified. "What's the matter with you? Hang onto him before he wakes up everybody in that burial mound!"

"You get him!" Gonzales was still shaking his injured hand. I'm not putting *my* hand over his mouth again and have it half bit off. I can tell you that right now!"

Red tried to wrestle Doug to the ground. "Shut him up or he'll have the whole village after us!"

With that Juan Gonzales seemed to realize the importance of stopping Doug's desperate screams for help. Gingerly he put his hand over the boy's mouth once more, clamping it so tightly he could not get it open to scream or bite.

"Do not bite me again or I will knock your head off!" Juan's whispered warning was ominous.

"Take it easy, kid!" Sanford said. "We ain't goin' to hurt you none if you do what we say. We just want to talk to you!"

At last, too exhausted to continue fighting any longer, Doug gave up. His youthful body sagged limply while he fought to breathe.

"There, now!" Red was panting heavily, too. It was plain to see that he was as weary as Doug. Only his extra weight and the increased strength that came with age had made it possible for him to overpower the boy – that and the help Gonzales gave him. "Get a vine, Juan! We've got to get this stubborn brat tied up."

"What're you going to do that for?" Doug demanded.

"We write a note to your old man about you!" Gonzales said.

"A note?"

"Sí. We get plenty of pesos from your millionaire papa for you."

"Shut up, Juan!" Red was firm and decisive. "Get him gagged and tied, will you? We've got things to do!"

* * *

In the clear place below, Del, Phil, and Mack stared at one another, wordlessly.

"Did you hear that?" Del cried.

"It sounds like someone grabbed Doug!"

"Come on!" Del cried, starting for the thick jungle where his brother had disappeared moments before. "What're we waiting for? We've got to help him!"

Phil Roper grabbed him by the arm. "Take it easy, man!" His voice was a whisper. "We can't help Doug that way!"

Del tried to jerk free, but his cousin tightened his grip on his wrist. "Take it easy, will you? If we all do something foolish and get caught, we won't do either Doug or ourselves any good."

Slowly Del's struggling ceased.

"What do you suppose happened to him?" he asked, numbly.

"I don't know, but it sounded to me as though somebody grabbed him and is going to keep him captive."

"But why?"

Phil shook his head. "Maybe this is the work of those bandits that tried to stop us yesterday."

Del straightened slowly. "Why would they do that?" he asked.

"To hold him for ransom, probably. At least that's as good a guess as any."

"But why? Danny and Kay don't have any money."

"Those guys who got Doug don't know that." Phil fell silent.

"What are we going to do?" his cousin asked. "There's no telling what they'll do to him, especially if they find out that Danny isn't rich enough to give them a lot of money to let him go."

Below, the boys from the village who had followed them up to place of the dead, had turned and bolted with Doug's first terror-stricken cry for help. Not one of them was in sight. But Del and his companions were so frightened they didn't even notice.

"W-w-what are we going to do?" Del asked again.

The muscles around Phil's mouth tightened. "We've got to get word to Dad as quickly as we can. That's the first thing."

"And that's not going to be easy. They've gone all the way to Monte and may be gone for a couple of days."

"Why don't you go back to the village, Mack? You speak Spanish a lot better than we do, and you know all the people. See if you can borrow a bicycle or a burro or something and get down to the city and catch Dad and your uncle. They'll know what to do."

Mack hesitated. "What about you guys?" His gaze shifted uneasily from one boy to the other. "What are you going to do?"

"We'll follow those guys and see if we can find out where they take Doug," Phil said.

Mack really wanted to go with his friends, but he knew the wisdom of getting word to his Uncle Felipe and Mr. Roper as quickly as possible. He turned obediently and sped down the steep path to the village. He was within sight of the abandoned church when he caught up with the guys from the village. Eduardo stared at him, eyes round with fright.

His younger brother, Pedro, was the first to speak. "We told you that the spirits would get angry if you dig in the place where the old ones are buried. We warned you, Mack, but you would not listen. Now all of your friends are gone." Eduardo shook his head sagely.

"That wasn't the spirits," Mack countered. "That was something else." His eyes darkened ominously. "Some men, I think. The same men who cut the tree so it fell across the road when we were coming up here yesterday."

But the boys were not listening to him.

"No, Mack," Eduardo continued, "It was nothing like that. It was the spirits. They were *mucho* angry when you dig in the graves of the old ones! And they punish you for it! They bring trouble to the Americanos because they are probably the ones who get you to do this terrible thing." And then Eduardo remembered something else, something Mack had told him before he decided that they should go up to the place of the dead to dig for pottery. "Or maybe they punish you for turning your back on the religion of our fathers!"

Mack was unconvinced. "If that's what it was, why wouldn't the spirits have punished me?" he asked. "I am the one who left the ways of our fathers."

The boys thought about that.

"They punish you by punishing your new friends first," he said, "or like I told you, maybe they punish the Americanos because they coax you to leave the old ways. But they will punish you, Mack, if you do not come back!"

Eduardo's companions nodded their complete agreement. Mack knew there was nothing to what Eduardo said, but he also knew that it would do no good for him to try to persuade them differently. They had already made up their minds that this was the reason for what happened.

Besides, Mack was too upset about Doug at the moment to be concerned about what his village friends were saying. He had to get down to his aunt's and see if she could help him get a bicycle or a burro so he could get to the city of Monte. Every minute counted.

* * *

Del and Phil were motionless for a time after Mack ran away. They stared uncertainly at each other.

"We've got to try and find where they're keeping Doug," Phil said, "but how are we going to go about it?"

"We'll have to try to follow them, that's all I know."

He nodded. "But we're going to have to keep our eyes open or they'll grab us, too. And then things will be even worse!"

"That's a chance we've got to take." His determination grew. "We've got to be careful enough to keep from getting caught."

Phil was still not sure that they had decided on the right move although the idea had originally been his.

"I'm not so sure this is the right thing to do, Del," he said, "now that I give it another thought or two. What are we going to do if Dad and Mack's Uncle Felipe come up here? How are they going to find us?"

"Search me." He drew himself up quickly. "I don't care how they find us! I'm going to follow those guys who've got Doug!"

"But–"

"You can do as you please, but I've got to help him get free if I can."

"Okay, okay," Phil said in resignation. "If you're determined to look for them, I'm going with you. But slow down a little, will you? We don't want them to catch us before we get started!"

* * *

Red Sanford was jerking Doug noisily up the steep slope.

"You guys are going to get in plenty of trouble for this," the American lad said. "You'll be thrown in jail for so long you'll forget what it's like being on the outside."

"Shut up!"

"Take it easy, Señor Red!" Gonzales warned. "Anyone within a mile of us can hear you!"

Sanford's laugh echoed brazenly through the still morning air.

"Those kids won't have enough nerve to follow us. Didn't you see them scatter?"

Juan nodded. "Sí, señor, I see them scatter all right, but I do not know if they stayed away or if they come sneaking back to follow us."

"We don't have to worry about those guys following us. We scared the pants off of them. What we've got to do now is to get far enough away so this kid's old man won't be able to find us."

Gonzales gasped. "You think maybe he look for us, señor? I thought you said he would pay the ransom pesos pronto!"

Red laughed again. "He'll pay off, all right, because that's the only way he's going to get the kid back. But there's a good chance he'll try to follow us first."

Gonzales stopped, the strength going out of his

muscular frame. "I don't think I like this, Señor Red. I don't like it at all."

Sanford exploded indignantly. "It don't make no difference to me whether you like it or not, see? You're in on this with me, and we're going through with it. Do you understand?"

Gonzales nodded. He could do nothing to take a chance on losing all those pesos. Sixteen burro-loads! A man had to take risks for a fortune like that.

"Sí," he managed. "I understand."

"Good. Then let's don't hear any more back talk off of you. Okay?"

* * *

Del and Phil crept stealthily through the all but impenetrable jungle, following Doug and his captors. The men who had kidnapped the Davis boy were so careless about breaking branches and leaving a trail that it would have been simple to track them. But that was not necessary. They could hear them plowing excitedly up the mountain without a thought about the noise they were making.

"Those guys sure must be stupid," Phil murmured as he and Del hurried along. "Listen to them. They sound like a herd of elephants going through the trees."

"As much noise as they're making, they must not think we would dare to follow them."

Phil slowed his pace momentarily. "I'm still not sure it's a good idea."

"You can go back if you want to," Del told him. "I'm going on."

"All right, if that's the way you feel about it. I just didn't want to make things worse by getting caught, that's all."

Del fell silent. His heart was pounding savagely, and he could scarcely breathe he was so frightened. He thought he was a lot more scared than Phil. But he couldn't stop. Not when his brother was in the clutches of those men ahead of them.

They had been making their way through the bush for some fifteen or twenty minutes without pausing when, suddenly, the noise ahead of them ceased. Phil stopped, listening, but there was no sound.

"What do you suppose happened to them?" he whispered tensely.

Del's cheeks were ashen, and sweat beaded his forehead. He licked his dry lips with the tip of his tongue.

The men who had grabbed Doug had stopped. That could mean they had reached their destination or–or– He didn't dare allow himself to think about the alternatives.

"Come on, Phil!" He spoke in a tense whisper but with great emotion. "We've got to find them!"

"Okay! But take it easy! We don't want them to find us!"

CHAPTER 10

ESCAPE STRATEGIES

Up the mountain about a hundred yards ahead of Del and Phil, Sanford and Gonzales stopped. Doug tried to jerk away.

"I warned you!" the American said and cursed angrily. "Try that again and I'll give you a clout you won't forget!"

"You'd better let me go or you won't be clouting anyone for the rest of your life. They'll throw you in jail that long!"

Juan Gonzales shuddered.

"What's the matter, Juan?" Doug taunted. "Don't you like being in jail?"

"Who said anything about being in jail?"

"That's where you're going. Back to jail. The law's rough on kidnappers, let me tell you."

"Shut your big mouth!"

The Mexican was eyeing Sanford quizzically.

"Why'd you tell him I'd been in jail?" he demanded. "Did you tell him you were there, too?"

"I didn't tell him nothin', but you have. Can't you ever learn to be quiet?"

Doug studied their faces. It had been a lucky guess that Gonzales had been in jail. He thought he had seen Juan react when he mentioned being locked up and figured that he had been in prison. If he could only get those two guys to squabble between themselves, he might be able to figure a way to get loose. While he was considering that possibility, Gonzales turned to Sanford, trying to keep from showing his own fright.

"Now what do we do, Señor Red?" he asked.

"We'll put him in that cave over there and write our ransom note to his old man." Red was in charge of the situation, and it was obvious that he was going to remain in control, if possible.

Doug realized this as he began to twist and squirm in his ropes.

"Now, señor, do not do that." Gonzales was almost apologetic. "We do not want to hurt you."

He continued to struggle against his bonds. Gonzales was watching him curiously. "What is it?" he asked. "What is the matter with you?"

"Stow the talk! We've got our work cut out for us!" He took a pencil stub from his pocket, along with a crumpled candy bar wrapper. "Sharpen this pencil for me so I can write our note and get it down to his old man."

"A lot of good it's going to do you to write that note," Doug said defiantly. "You aren't going to get anything out of anybody for me. You'd just as well know it right now."

Sanford's scowl darkened his ugly face. "You shut your big mouth! When I want to hear from you, I'll tell you! Understand?"

Doug laughed in spite of the situation in which he found himself.

"Maybe you'd better listen to what I've got to tell you," Doug continued. "You aren't *that* stupid, are you?"

Sanford cocked his fist and gestured menacingly with it.

"You know what you characters have done?" He laughed again. "You made the biggest mistake of your lives in grabbing me. Nobody's going to pay you any ransom to get *me* back!"

Gonzales gasped. "What do you mean?"

"He's just tryin' to feed you a line, Juan. Don't pay any attention to him!"

Doug's laugh was scornful. "You've got the wrong guy, that's what I mean."

Gonzales grabbed him roughly by the shoulder. In his agitation he squeezed harder than he meant to. "What you say, boy?"

"My father isn't the one who's with us. My father's

been dead for a long time. So you got the wrong guy if you think you're going to get a lot of money for me."

"You hear that, Señor Red?" Gonzales was frantic. "You hear what he say? We got the wrong boy! The Señor Millionaire no give us five million pesos for somebody else's son! And that's for sure!"

"Five million pesos!" Doug had been taunting them, but his surprise at the size of the ransom they were asking was genuine. "You've got to be kidding! Nobody's going to give you five million pesos for me! I can tell you that right now!"

"Shut up!" Sanford gestured menacingly at Doug with his fist once more. "You aren't going to fool me with talk like that! I've seen you with your old man enough to know that you're his kid. So don't try to give us that stuff!"

"If you've seen me with my dad," Doug countered, "you must have seen me with him in Guatemala a long time ago. He was a missionary down there until he and my mother were drowned. Now we live in Minnesota with a man by the name of Danny Orlis."

Gonzales' eye narrowed. What the boy said had the ring of truth in it. He knew Red Sanford was supposed to be the one with the brains for this sort of thing and he shouldn't doubt him. But he had talked with men and boys enough himself to have a good idea when someone was trying to tell him something that wasn't true. There weren't many who could lie so convincingly.

"What is this–this missionary you say your father was?" he asked.

Before Doug could reply, Red stormed over to them.

"Both of you, shut up! I don't want to hear any more out of either of you!" He turned to face Doug. "You'll never make me believe that your old man isn't the one who drives the big car, so just quit tryin'."

The boy shrugged indifferently. "Suit yourself. You'll find out soon enough."

* * *

Clarence Roper and Felipe Flores finished their business in Monte that day and were starting toward home. The slight, dark-skinned villager was smiling happily.

"Imagine!" he exclaimed. "Ten times as much for the bowls and little clay figures as the man used to give us when he came to The Congregation of the Bulls." Wonder glinted in his eyes. "It is going to mean much to our village, señor. It will mean that we will have the money we need for clothes and food and medicine. How do we ever say thank you?"

"You don't have to thank me," he said. "I'm only glad that I was able to help you and your people."

"How did you know about this thing?" Felipe asked presently. "How did you know the pieces of clay were so valuable?"

"I didn't know it for sure, but I figured there had

to be some reason the American would come all the way down here and buy the pieces from you. I'm glad we found out the truth."

They rode on for a mile or more in silence.

"This I do not understand," Mack's uncle continued after some thought. "You come to us a stranger, but you take your time and your nice car to do this thing for us." He touched the Texan's arm. "Why, Señor Roper? Is there something you want from us?"

Clarence knew why he asked that question. The only Americans he saw were those who wanted to get something from him or his people. They took advantage – like the one who came and bought the artifacts for a fraction of what they were actually worth.

"No, Felipe. There is nothing I want from you. I have not come to get anything from you for myself."

Mr. Flores shook his head. He wanted to believe this tall Americano who spoke with such a soft, straightforward voice and who always wore such a smile. But it was hard to be sure that this one was any different than the others, that this one was not going to take advantage of him.

Clarence Roper knew what he must be thinking. "A year ago, Felipe," he said, "I would have been just like the man who came down to buy those bowls and figures from you. I'd have taken every advantage of you that I could if it would have made me any money. But something happened to me that changed all of that."

His companion leaned forward curiously. This was something that he had not heard before, that something could happen to a man to change him, so he was no longer greedy.

"Yes?"

"I met the Lord Jesus Christ. I confessed my sin and asked Him to change my life. And He did."

Felipe's lean face grew serious. "This I do not understand."

"I didn't understand it either at first. All I knew was that it was true." Clarence went on to tell his new friend how all men are wicked and deserve to go to hell. "But God loved us so much He didn't want to have us lost and apart from Him, so He sent His Son to save us."

Felipe nodded as though he knew what Clarence was talking about, but it was quite obvious that he didn't. The Texas rancher drove on, praying silently. It was so hard for someone like himself, who hadn't learned anything about the Bible as a kid, to talk to a man like the one who sat beside him. He couldn't answer his questions, that was sure. He wished he knew the Bible like Danny Orlis did or the brother-in-law he used to dislike so fervently. Then he might be able to find the words to say that would help Felipe find Christ as his Savior.

* * *

Red Sanford laboriously finished printing his note on the candy wrapper. Doug, who was watching with obvious amusement, said nothing. The squat Mexican, Gonzales, paced back and forth, talking about the sixteen burro-loads of pesos he was going to get as his share of the ransom money.

"Listen to this, Gonzales." Red cleared his throat and read the note aloud.

> We have your kid. If you don't come across with five million pesos pronto, you will never see him again. In our next note, we will send instructions for getting the money to us.
>
> (Signed) The Avengers

Gonzales, who had been listening to the note with approval, jerked upright as his companion finished.

"'The Avengers'?" he exclaimed, his eyes widening. "And who are the avengers, Señor Red?"

The American swore fervently. "That's you and me, stupid!"

"I don't know if I like that name. It might make the Señor Millionaire mad at us."

Sanford snorted his derision. "I don't know why I had to end up with such a dumb partner on an important deal like this. 'Who are the avengers?' How ignorant can you be?"

Juan Gonzales sat down, completely unconcerned.

It didn't bother him that Red kept calling him names. He was used to that by this time. He knew his companion didn't mean what he said. And even if he had meant it, it would not have mattered to the Mexican. He didn't care that much about Red one way or the other.

Sanford folded the note carefully and came over to where Gonzales was sitting.

"I want you to take this down to the village and see that the American gets it."

He looked up. "One minute, señor. If you think I am going into the village, you can guess again. I am not going up to him and say, 'Señor Millionaire, we have your son back in the jungle. Here is a note about it.' You do your own going to the village if you want it done. That is where I stop."

Sanford shook his head as though to emphasize how foolish Juan Gonzales was.

"I don't want any more trouble from you, Gonzales. If you want your share of the five million pesos, you've got to do something to earn it."

"Okay. I stay here and guard the kid. You deliver the note."

"Take this note and go down near the village, Gonzales, and hide in the brush. When some kid comes along, you give them the note and tell them to give it to the American. That's all there is to it."

"If it's so easy, why don't you do it?"

"Because you're Mexican and speak Spanish,

that's the reason. If a kid from the village saw me, the chances are that he'd turn and run away."

Juan's concern did not vanish with Sanford's assurance that the task was simple. "I take the note, Señor Red," he said, "and I deliver it like you say, but I don't think I'm going to like it."

* * *

Phil and Del were painstakingly making their way up the mountain when Juan Gonzales started down. They heard him coming an instant before he burst into view.

"Get down!" Phil ordered in a harsh whisper.

Quickly they dropped to their stomachs in the lush undergrowth. And just in time. Gonzales passed by so close that either of them could have reached out and touched him had they wanted to.

When he was finally gone, Del sat up slowly. "That was close!"

"You can say that again!"

"I thought he was going to step on one of us. We were lucky he didn't."

Del got to his feet as quietly as possible.

"You know, I just thought of something. There's one less guard up there watching Doug now! This might be our chance."

Excitement continued to grip them with tightening fingers as they crept stealthily upward. They parted the heavy ferns and brush with great care and eased themselves up the mountain a step at a time. Phil turned to his cousin to whisper his uneasiness.

"I wish we knew where Doug and that bandit are," he said. "I'd hate to stumble onto them."

The other boy held a finger to his mouth in warning.

Three or four steps ahead were screened by heavy undergrowth. Beyond, there was a little clearing. They eased forward cautiously until they were close enough to see the sheer rock cliff a dozen paces or so away that shoved upward toward the sky. At its base Del saw Red Sanford sprawled on the ground, eyes closed. Beyond him was the mouth of the cave.

"There they are!" Del's whispers were taut with emotion. "Doug's in that cave!"

"And there's only one guy guarding him!"

Del and Phil stared questioningly at each other. They hadn't realized they would get an opportunity like this, but they weren't sure what action they ought to take.

"What do we do now?" Phil's lips scarcely formed the words.

"We've got to get Doug away from him before that other character gets back!"

"And just exactly how do we do that?"

He hesitated uneasily. He didn't know for sure how they were going to be able to free Doug. All he knew was that they had to do it. A prayer welled in his heart as he looked at the dimly outlined form of his brother.

CHAPTER 11

NEW CAPTIVES FOR CHRIST

Mack had borrowed a donkey in the village and had ridden two or three miles along the mountain road toward the highway and Monte when Mr. Roper and his uncle met him. He waved wildly as soon as he saw them rounding the curve ahead of him. Clarence braked to a halt.

"Mack!" he exclaimed. "Where are you going?"

Excitedly the boy blurted out the story. Felipe Flores was as frightened as his young nephew when he heard that Doug had been kidnapped.

"Who did this thing, Mack?" he demanded. "Who is responsible for this terrible wrong to our friends?"

The boy shook his head. "I do not know. One minute we were digging at the place of the dead and the next–"

Felipe cried aloud. "The place of the dead? You dig *there*?"

"Sí. To get the things the man wants to buy, we dug with our machetes."

Slowly Felipe turned to Clarence, fear deeply etched in his thin features.

"It is the spirits who do this, señor. For many years our fathers and our fathers' fathers have warned us about molesting the place of the dead. And always our people have obeyed – until now! I am most sorry, señor, but there is nothing anyone can do to help. It is the work of the spirits!"

Mr. Roper broke in decisively. "Nonsense! I don't know what has happened to Doug any more than you do, but I can tell you right now that the spirits didn't have anything to do with it. This has got to be the work of men!"

Mr. Flores disagreed, but he did not argue with his new friend. How could he, when Señor Roper had been so good to him and the others in The Congregation of the Bulls?

Clarence was silent for a moment or two. "I'll hurry up to the village with you and then go back to Monte for the police," he said. "This is a matter for them to attend to!"

When the car drove into the village, a small boy came running up to the car. "Señor Americano! Señor Americano!" His voice trembled with importance. "I have to talk to you right away."

Clarence was about to ignore the lad who was

hurrying in his direction, but something about the urgency in his voice caused him to stop.

"Yes?"

The boy blurted out to him in staccato Spanish that lost Clarence in the first few words.

"What did he say, Felipe?"

"He says he was playing on the edge of the woods when a man came up to him and gave him this piece of paper. He told him it was *mucho* important and that he should take it to you immediately and not give it to anyone else."

Roper snatched the piece of paper from the ragged boy's hand and stared at it. His face whitened, and his breath came in a tortured gasp.

"The character who wrote this can't be serious. It's got to be some kind of a joke!"

"What is it, señor?"

"A ransom note, I guess!" He read it aloud. "Somebody must have thought Doug was my own son. At any rate, they've kidnapped him and are going to hold him until I pay them five million pesos!"

Felipe stood up tall. "Five million pesos? I did not know there was so much money in all of Mexico!"

"I don't have that much, that's for sure."

Felipe's concern for the kidnapped boy was almost as great as that of Clarence's. He sat motionless in the car, his gaze riveted to his companion's face.

"What do we do, señor? How do we get him back?"

"I'm still going down for the police! That's the first thing to do."

"I stay here!" Felipe had made up his mind what he and the men in the settlement could do. "I get my friends and we go out and look for this boy. Nobody knows the mountain the way we do. If he is here, we find him, señor."

Clarence hesitated. He didn't know whether it was wise to go out and look for Doug and his captors or not. In a way he was afraid of what the men might do to their hostage if they found out that someone was after them. Yet he had prayed about it, and this seemed to be an answer.

"Fine, my friend. Be careful that you don't cause them to get so scared they–they try to do something to him."

Felipe shook Clarence's hand in a quick gesture of understanding and friendship.

* * *

Up on the mountain Del and Phil watched Sanford carefully from their hiding place in the jungle. He had stretched out on the ground and closed his eyes. Doug was still pestering him.

"Juan probably knows the truth by now," he taunted, "or he will in a little while. Then you'll know that you've got the wrong guy."

"Shut up, will you? I'm goin' to take a nap."

"They'll soon tell him I'm not the guy you should've kidnapped. You'll find out that I'm not Mr. Roper's son and that you're more stupid than Juan."

Sanford gestured menacingly at him. "Shut up, will you? I want to get a little sleep."

Del poked his cousin in the ribs. "Right now I'm like that guy. I wish Doug'd shut up and let him go to sleep."

The kidnapped boy was still muttering to himself but so softly the boys in the brush were unable to hear him. He didn't seem to be disturbing the man who was guarding him, however. At least he rolled over on his side and closed his eyes. In a minute or two he was snoring softly.

Phil turned to his companion. "There! He's finally gone to sleep. I didn't think he'd do it."

"Neither did I." They were talking in excited whispers. "But whatever we do, we've got to do it quickly. There's no knowing when he's going to wake up or his buddy is going to come back."

"Or when that brother of yours will wake him!"

Del and Phil used their machetes to cut a length of vine that was hanging from a nearby tree. Del coiled it in his hand, and, taking his machete in the other hand, he began to creep through the jungle, working his way closer to the sleeping man before coming out in the open. Phil was right behind him. They were just ready to step from the brush when Doug spoke up loudly.

"Red! Red!" His voice reverberated through the jungle.

Del and Phil both groaned. "What's the matter with him, anyway?" Phil whispered.

Sanford grunted and opened his eyes.

"Shut up, will you?"

"Juan's going to be back in a little while. What're you going to do with me when you find out that you've kidnapped the wrong kid?"

"If you don't shut up, I'll skin you and hang you up to dry before Juan gets back. How would you like that?" He closed his eyes once more.

That was the instant Del and Phil had been waiting for. They leaped from the jungle, ignoring the noise they were making, and bounded across the cleared spot to where Sanford was lying. The American opened his eyes and stared at them, frozen for an instant by the sudden onslaught. Then he scrambled to his feet.

"Don't do that!" Del held the machete in both hands like a baseball bat.

Red crouched motionless, fear dulling his eyes. "You–you wouldn't use that," he whimpered.

"Don't be too sure!"

Sanford jerked his head to see another machete, held by Phil, poised ominously over him.

"I–I wasn't goin' to hurt him. Honest, I wasn't. It was the other guy's idea to hold him for ransom," he pleaded. "I was just goin' to scare him a little and turn him loose."

"Don't let him kid you!" Doug exclaimed. "Red's the planner. He told me so himself!'

Del tossed the vine to Phil. "Tie him up. I'll see that he doesn't try any funny stuff."

By this time the little courage the American had was gone. He was blubbering for mercy.

"I'm not going to try anything. Put that machete down. You–you might get scared or something and–and hurt somebody without meaning to!"

The boys herded Sanford into the cave and tied him securely with his hands behind his back. They used another piece of vine to tie his feet so he could only take the smallest of steps.

"Now come over here and get me loose, will you? Juan's going to be back any minute, and you're going to need my help," Doug called.

Del grinned. "If we did what we ought to, we'd leave you tied up for a while. You just about spoiled everything. I suppose you know that."

Before Doug could answer they heard a noise in the jungle below them. Doug jerked his hands free as his brother cut the rope that bound them.

"It's him! Juan Gonzales is coming!"

The Davis boys and Phil crouched tensely in the semidarkness of the cave, their breathing shallow and rapid.

"Señor Red!" Gonzales' voice boomed across the jungle and into the cave. "Señor Red! I take the note to that Señor Millionaire. And before I leave, I see his car go down the mountain. He go to get our five million pesos, I betcha!"

Gonzales must have reached the open space by this time. The sound of his running stopped suddenly.

"Señor Red!" Fear laced his voice. "Señor Red! Where are you?"

Gonzales' questions loosed the other man's voice.

"Run before they get you, too!"

Juan's mind worked rapidly enough on occasion, but this time he did not believe his companion.

"Oh, no, Señor Red! You do not get rid of me so easy now that we are about to get our five million pesos. I come into the cave and stay with you, just like we planned. Half of that money is mine!"

"Run!" Desperation laced Sanford's tones. "Get out of here before it's too late!"

Gonzales laughed. "You make the joke, no?"

With that he started into the cave, blinking in the sudden darkness.

"You shouldn't try to fool me, Señor Red. That isn't nice to do."

Sanford groaned in desperation. "You big ox! Why didn't you run while you had the chance? Now they'll get you, too!"

At that instant Del and Doug swarmed over the startled Mexican. Phil held his machete over their captive to keep him from using the confusion to try and get away. Gonzales was short but powerfully built. They would never have been able to throw him to the ground had it not been for the advantage of surprise. He fought valiantly, but they were able to get a length of the vine wrapped about his arms and pin them securely to his sides.

"What you do?" Gonzales demanded plaintively. "I never do nothing to you, Señor Red. Why you treat me this way?"

Sanford growled his denial. "What do you mean, why do *I* treat you this way? They've got me tied up too!"

"That's right!" Doug was panting heavily from the exertion. "I told you guys that you'd never get away with it!"

Juan's eyes widened. "You don't tell me we got company, Señor."

"I tried to, but you wouldn't listen."

"I–I–" Gonzales' lips worked frantically but no sounds came out.

The Davis boys got to their feet. "Okay, Juan. Let's get up and get with it. We've got quite a walk ahead of us!"

Gonzales licked his lips. "Where you taking us?"

"To the village first and then to jail."

Juan groaned. "Are you really going to let them do that, Señor Red?"

Sanford did not answer.

* * *

The boys came marching into the village triumphantly an hour later, pushing Red Sanford and Juan
Gonzales ahead of them.

"It is them!" A shrill cry went up as they came down
the steep slope past the crumbling church building.
"It is the boys! The spirits do not get them after all!"

A head popped curiously out of the nearest mud
and stick house. A moment later there were faces
peering from every doorway.

Doug touched Sanford between the shoulder
blades with his finger. "Look pretty," he said softly,
"you're a celebrity now."

"Shut up, will you?"

"And another thing. When Uncle Clarence gets
back, I want you to ask him if I'm his son. I want
you to know how dumb you were kidnapping me
and trying to get money out of him to get me back."

It wasn't long after the boys reached the village
plaza that Clarence Roper and two carloads of police-
men came roaring into the middle of town. Clarence
saw the boys as he braked to a halt.

"Doug!" His shout sounded above the noise of
the crowd. "Are you all right?"

The boy grinned. "Sure, I'm all right. I'm fine.
Our friends here don't feel so good, though. I don't
think they're too happy to see the men you brought
with you."

Everyone was laughing and talking at once as
the police untied Red Sanford and Juan Gonzales,

handcuffed them securely, and loaded them into one of the vehicles. Then the officer in charge came over to the boys.

"Now, we are going to have to find out from you exactly what happened." He spoke in broken English. "You will come in to our office on your way back to the States, won't you?"

Clarence answered for them. "I'll see that they do. We're going to have to be on our way in a day or two."

The officer thanked the boys profusely, said goodbye to Clarence Roper, and turned back toward Monte.

That night Mr. Roper had an opportunity to talk with Felipe and his wife and family about their need to make a commitment of their lives to Christ.

"Sí, what you say talks to my heart, señor." Felipe paused significantly. "But only because you talk to me with your life first."

Clarence stared at him incredulously. At first he didn't realize what his new Mexican friend was trying to say. Felipe read the question in his eyes.

"You and the boys come among us as friends," he explained. "You try to help us. You don't try to make money on us because we do not know the value of the things that are ours. And even before that, you take my brother's wife and family onto your ranch. You give them a good place to live. You see that they have what they need to eat. You treat them the way you would want your own family treated. If this is what it means to be a Christian, señor, then that is what I want for myself and my family. I want my life to speak for me the way yours speaks for you."

There were tears in Mr. Roper's eyes as he got out his Bible and began to explain to Felipe and his family exactly how they could commit their lives to the Lord Jesus Christ.

* * *

"Well," Clarence said as they headed the car toward Monte and home, "the Lord answered your prayers for your relatives, Mack. Eduardo and his parents are Christians now."

"Sí." The boy's face was thoughtful. "But there are some of my friends who do not have Jesus as their Savior yet. I try to tell them about Him, but they no listen."

"We'll have to keep praying for them," the rancher told him. "We'll ask God to use your Uncle Felipe and Eduardo to help them see that they, too, need Jesus."

They passed the tree that Gonzales and Sanford had cut down and put across the road. Doug and Del grinned as they saw it.

"It's been a great trip, hasn't it?"

"You can say that again," Phil answered.

THE
DANNY ORLIS
SERIES

The Danny Orlis series, by Bernard Palmer, delivers a blend of adventure, mystery, and suspense through various settings—from the Canadian wilderness to Guatemalan jungles. Danny Orlis, an adept outdoorsman, skilled athlete, and committed Christian, employs his quick thinking, calm bravery, and biblical solutions to confront everyday problems and hair-raising dangers. Early stories focus on Danny navigating school life, sports, and outdoor challenges, while in later books, Danny and his wife Kay provide wisdom and guidance to youngsters facing lifelike situations and challenges. Having sold over two million copies, this series has made Palmer a renowned author in Christian youth literature. Palmer is also the author of the Felicia Cartright series and various other series for Christian youth.

AVAILABLE FROM WWW.ANEKOPRESS.COM